VIOLET'S VOW

A Botanical Seasons Novella: Book Two

Jenny Knipfer

Jenny Knipfer © 2022

Violet's Vow
Copyright © 2022 Jenny Knipfer
All rights reserved.

No part of this book may be reproduced or stored in any information storage system without prior written consent of the publisher or the author, except in the case of brief quotations with proper references.

Cover design by Historical Fiction Book Covers, Jenny Q.
Editing by Sara Litchfield
Formatting by Polgarus Studio.

ISBN: 978-1-7379575-1-5
Printed in the United States of America

Disclaimer: This is a work of fiction. Similarities to real people, places, and events are purely coincidental.

JENNY'S OTHER BOOKS

BY THE LIGHT OF THE MOON SERIES:
Ruby Moon
Blue Moon
Silver Moon
Harvest Moon

SHELTERING TREES SERIES:
In a Grove of Maples
Under the Weeping Willow
On Bur Oak Ridge

BOTANICAL SEASONS NOVELLA SERIES:
Holly's Homecoming

Praise for the
By the Light of the Moon series

"*Readers who love being trapped in a character's mind should relish this finely written, gripping series. A must read for fans of historical fiction.*" The Prairies Book Review

Ruby Moon

"*This novel is filled with drama and a writing style that is insightful. From the beginning, the author creates a sense of mystery, capturing sensations in a style that defies perception.*" Readers' Favorite, five-star review

"*Knipfer's characterization is stellar in this novel, and she skillfully ties in the themes of faith, forgiveness, and trust.*" Wisconsin Writers Association

"*Ruby Moon is the type of book that hooks you from page one… and has you quickly turning the pages to discover more.*" Ya It's Lit Blog

"*The prose is just beautiful with a lyricism that ebbs and flows perfectly. I love a story that sounds to me like a song.*" Jypsy Lynn

"Jenny is a talented wordsmith who knows how to be creative and brazen with her thoughts and think outside of the box. I adore how Jenny took risks with Ruby Moon and decided to put a twist on a much-loved genre…"
The Red Headed Book Lover

"It does not always happen but when it does it feels miraculous. I'm talking about when you read a book and you are immersed in it. I started to read the first page… and when I got to the last page, I closed the book and held it to my heart." Linda McCutcheon, book blogger and reviewer

Blue Moon

"Knipfer creates a strong sense of place, and she draws on her own experience with MS to depict the course of Valerie's illness with great sensitivity." Wisconsin Writers Association

"Blue Moon continues a well-written and highly engaging saga of family ties, betrayals, and heartaches. A must-read for historical drama fans everywhere." Readers' Favorite, five-star review

"In Blue Moon, the author tells a breathtaking story of twins Vanessa and Valerie. Page after page, the author masterfully weaves other exciting characters into the story…"
Ksenia Sein, author of Agape & Ares

"Knipfer continues to welcome her readers into Webaashi Bay… back into the town and characters we fell in love with… For in this book, Knipfer has woven an entrancing tale we all need to hear." Amazon reviewer

Silver Moon

"Silver Moon is a highly recommended read for fans of historical wartime fiction, powerful emotive drama, and excellent atmospheric writing." Readers' Favorite, five-star review

"I am stunned by the amount of detail the author gave in this single story. On one hand, we have powerful characters… and on the other, we have a plot that demands all our attention. Jenny Knipfer pulls no punches and holds nothing back." Readers' Favorite, five-star review

"This story felt comfortable for a first-time reader to the author, more like being welcomed by new friends. The setting, a time of need, camaraderie and survival, brings the large cast and reader together. Ultimately, Silver Moon *is a story of forgiveness, second chances, prayer and patience."* Wisconsin Writers Association

"Silver Moon is very highly recommended for readers who want a compelling inspection of love, duty, and battle based on historical fact, but flavored with the struggles of very different characters intent on not just surviving but

creating a better future for themselves." D. Donovan, Midwest Book Review

"Taking an original angle on a tumultuous time in history, Silver Moon *by Jenny Knipfer is a sparkling slice of historical fiction. Rather than focusing solely on the violence of this tragic conflict, Knipfer fleshes out the complexity of wartime... a thought-provoking and surprising work of historical escapism."* Self-Publishing Review

"Not a light-hearted read, this book will engulf your senses, evoking the deepest and highest of emotions as you cheer and cry for the survival of dearly loved characters." Kathryn V. Goodreads review

Harvest Moon

"As in her prior books, Jenny Knipfer does an outstanding job of cementing place, time, and culture against the backdrop of evolving relationships. These approaches lend a solid feel of authenticity and attraction to her plot to keep readers both educated and engrossed, as spiritual and social matters evolve." D. Donovan, Midwest Book Review

"Wielding descriptive language and unexpected imagery, this narrative transports a reader with ease. Harvest Moon *is a moving, authentic, and original work of historical fiction, while this series is a testament to Knipfer's skilled and versatile storytelling."* Self-Publishing Review

"Harvest Moon *by Jenny Knipfer is one of the best books I have read in 2020. In fact, it is probably one of the best historical fiction novels I have ever read. I have come away deep in thought, feeling somewhat like I've had a mystical experience and one I will never forget.*" Viga Boland, Readers' Favorite, five-star review

"*The author created the perfect atmosphere for her story to truly bloom and progress. I would highly recommend this historical fiction novel to anyone who loves reading stories with intricate plots and powerful characters.*" Rabina Tanveer, Readers' Favorite, five-star review

"*Knipfer creates her characters with so much emotion and physical presence that they become almost real in the imagination. A captivating and evocative novel of the importance of family, faith, and forgiveness and how, together, those things help heal a broken heart.*" Gloria Bartel, Wisconsin Writers Association

"*It is also a powerful story of strength and survival and of love and forgiveness. A memorable read.*" *New York Times* Bestselling Author Lorena McCourtney

"Harvest Moon *is a gripping story told through flashbacks and a split timeline. Knipfer is quite skilled at creating lively characters that drew me right in.*" Regina Walker, author of *We Go On* and *Still With Us*

Praise for the *Sheltering Trees* series

In a Grove of Maples

"... *a heartfelt tale of the struggles of married life on a nineteenth-century farm. Edward and Beryl are both relatable and sympathetic. Knipfer expertly captures the emotion and stress of their lives and relationship. It's a touching and realistic portrayal of love, loss, and friendship.*" Heather Stockard, Readers' Favorite, five-star review

"*Dramatic character development and lavish descriptive language make Knipfer's prose shine and carry this emotionally stirring plot from start to finish. The storytelling is casual but unmistakably aged, and the research into this particular time period is remarkable, while the variation in narrative format keeps the story engaging throughout.*" Self-Publishing Review

"*Readers of women's fiction and Christian historical romance will find* In a Grove of Maples *an engrossing story of 19th century rural life that examines matters of heart, ethics, morality, and belief as Beryl faces a new world with few resources other than her faith and love. It concludes with an unexpected twist that comes full circle to leave the door open for more.*" D. Donavon, Midwest Book Review

Under the Weeping Willow

"*A heart-rending, emotionally packed love story between a mother and daughter, Under the Weeping Willow is a journey of loss and brokenness coupled with forgiveness and healing. This time-split novel captured my heart and didn't release it until the final page. Beautiful and haunting, Robin and Enid's story swept me to another era. These characters lived, and I loved watching them find their way to each other. Keep the tissues handy. You don't want to miss this story!*" Candace West, Selah award finalist and author of the Valley Creek Redemption series

"*A gorgeous storyteller, Jenny Knipfer has the gift of blending strong imagery with vivid emotions to capture readers' hearts in this spellbinding story.*" Christian Sia for Readers' Favorite, five-star review

"*A sensitive and well-crafted drama unpacking issues of mental health, layers of grief, societal expectations, and the instability of memory, this novel is touching on the surface, but subtly and profoundly layered with meaning.*" Self-Publishing Review, five-star review

"*You don't have to be a fan of Christian historical fiction or family dramas to like this novel. Knipfer has created a story that crosses many genres and will appeal to those who love poignant epics about complex characters, engrossing plots, relatable situations, and a satisfying ending.*" Tammy Ruggles for Readers' Favorite, five-star review

Praise for the *Botanical Seasons* novella series

Holly's Homecoming

"Knipfer weaves a historical novella that offers twists and turns you'll never see coming, only to tie up this lovely holiday tale with a bright red bow. As always, the prose is nearly poetic —Knipfer's great skill, and it makes reading a delight. The characters are well thought out and not simple cut-outs — a difficult feat considering this is a novella and not a full-length historical." Jenny Cary, author of the inspirational series: *Relentless*, *The Crockett Chronicles*, and *The Weather Girls*

"A perfect short historical read for the busy season. Author Jenny Knipfer delivers a warm and festive story with a twist of mystery. I adored the ambience! Readers looking for their next favorite holiday novella will not want to miss Holly's Homecoming." Naomi Musch, author of fifteen novels including Selah and Book-of-the-Year finalist *Mist O'er the Voyageur*, the sequel *Song for the Hunter*, and the *Lumberjacks and Ladies* novella collection.

In memory of my Aunt Eleanor and Grandma M.,
both of whom loved flowers.
And for my friend Lacy, who taught me
much about floral design.

If thou of fortune be bereft,
and in my store there be but left,
two loaves, sell one,
and with the dole,
buy hyacinths to feed thy soul.

John Greenleaf Whittier

CHAPTER ONE

May 1891

Fluffing out the head of the peach-colored carnation in her hand, an envy built in Violet for the simplicity of the clove-scented flower. But although the fragrance held sweetness, carnations were said to have sprung up from Mary's tears along the path Jesus trod as He carried His cross. And thus, it was a divine flower, birthed in passion.

Though far removed from what the Lord suffered, Violet knew a bit about spent passion and wondered if her hopes and dreams would end up buried with Roger.

She brought the ruffled carnation petals to her nose, closing her eyes and breathing deeply. The spicy scent reminded her of the aftershave he had worn.

Dear Rodger—her best friend, confidant, and husband. She conjured his rugged yet handsome face in her mind: wide-set, brown eyes, a heavy brow, and deep lines around his mouth, from too many days in the sun. How she missed him still. Though his passing had been over a year ago, in some ways, it seemed like yesterday. They had been such good companions, interested in the same things, but Violet hadn't really considered them to be a love match. Theirs had been more a union of like minds, and oddly enough, their relationship had satisfied them both.

The bell tinkled on the shop door, and Violet stood to attention, rolling her eyes open to see who had entered her domain—Fragrant Sentiments. She and Roger had worked so hard to establish the flower shop, providing most of the cut flowers from their three greenhouses and multiple gardens. It had been full-time work just growing the flowers, let alone selling them, until they had hired Webster, a young man unafraid of hard work and eager to learn more about gardening. The three of them had made a happy team. However, they were three no longer, and the workload, at times, overwhelmed her. Whether she could keep the business afloat without Roger remained to be seen.

Violet keenly missed Roger's presence in the shop. Oddly enough for a man, he'd had an eye for design and arrangements of a grander scale, while it was the everyday bouquets that spoke to Violet. Her heart lay in the little treasures to brighten the home. She held to the philosophy that flowers should be an everyday part of a household, as much as tea or coffee were. Her Aunt Dahlia had often said that flowers were the morning drink of the soul, and Violet agreed.

Violet positioned the carnation next to some lilacs in a white, porcelain urn which held a half-arranged bouquet of flowers, destined for the funeral of a young woman. Finally focusing on her clientele, Violet's gaze brushed over the tailored cut of the man's light gray suit and the fine, couture lines of the light blue, silk dress the young woman wore. A loose pompadour style encapsulated her dark hair, and her dark brown eyes glistened like dewy centers of a rudbeckia.

The woman smiled, easy and sincere, showing straight teeth. "A good morning to you, ma'am. My, it smells so lovely in here."

She turned her head left and right, taking in the shop displays and buckets of flowers.

Violet offered a slight curve of her lips in return. "Thank you."

A tinge of envy nudged at Violet. She had lost that sense of identifying an overpowering, welcoming fragrance upon entering the flower shop some time ago, and she missed it. Her nose had gotten used to so many flowers in one space.

The young woman loosened the blue, velvet pouch

3

dangling from her wrist and pulled out a calling card. "I'm Miss Holly Moore, and this is my uncle, Mr. Devon Moore."

She flipped her wrist in the man's direction. He smiled, sincere as well but with a hint of something else altogether. *Sadness perhaps.* Upon that intuition, Violet instinctively glimpsed his spirit as a purple hyacinth, holding regret and sorrow. She had a way about her, for matching flowers to people.

Inclining his head ever so slightly, he said, "Ma'am," in an airy but not unmasculine voice.

Reaching out to take the card, Violet said, "Why, good day. I'm Mrs. Violet Brooks. How may I be of service to you?"

Meeting the young woman's dark eyes, fringed with lashes of the same dark shade, Violet marveled at Miss Moore's loveliness and sighed that her own medium brown hair was now streaked with gray. The mirror, of late, revealed how the smooth skin on her face had started to crease, and dappled age spots bloomed here and there on the backs of her hands and at her hairline.

Miss Moore flashed another smile at Violet. "I am planning a wedding in late June and would like to know what you might have available and what you could make for arrangements, as well as several bouquets."

Mr. Moore stood by silently, but he appeared attentive, his gaze trained on his niece, as if he feared she might disappear.

Violet didn't begrudge Miss Moore her happiness,

but oh how she worried over her own.

"Congratulations," she got out, despite the taste of gall in the back of her throat when she thought of how Roger had been taken from her, and with him their plans of expansion for Fragrant Sentiments. The vow she had made to seek out the man or men responsible and make them pay for their crime floated to the surface of her mind, begging to be realized, but she buried it again.

Violet sensed Miss Moore waited for her to speak.

Clearing her throat, she banished the taste of bitterness from her mouth and answered, "Well, that greatly depends on your preference and whether or not the sentimental value and the meaning behind the flowers is important to you."

Miss Moore batted her thick lashes. "Goodness, I hadn't really thought about that. But I do love roses."

"We may have a few varieties in bloom in June, but if you don't care for those, I could possibly have some roses shipped in. But I warn you. They will be expensive."

Violet swung her gaze to Mr. Moore.

Mr. Moore showered a loving look on Miss Moore, who met his gaze and blushed. "Spare no expense, Mrs. Brooks. I have but one niece."

Miss Moore laid the crocheted lace of her gloved hand on Mr. Moore's forearm. "Uncle Devon, you spoil me."

The statement would have been coy on most women's tongues, but Violet could tell Miss Moore spoke with sincerity and shared a true affection with her uncle. She appeared to be nothing like her botanical namesake—holly. Pretty but prickly, it was Violet's least favorite green to handle, and she always wore gloves when she did. No, Violet saw Miss Holly Moore as a blush pink lily—pretty and exemplifying femininity, hidden intuition, and an attractive charisma—an altogether pleasant persona.

"Nonsense. It is nothing more than you deserve," Mr. Moore told his niece, his salt and brown pepper mustache spreading wider along with his lips.

A well-shaped and clipped goatee connected his mustache around his chin. His cheeks, although holding the thicker flesh of a middle-aged man, did not sag into jowls but firmly arched back to his temples, where hair lighter than the color of his mustache curled underneath the edges of his straw hat, adorned with a band matching his suit. Altogether, Violet had to admit he cut a handsome figure of a man.

Moore. The name seemed familiar to her. She lowered her eyes from taking in Mr. Moore and studied the ivory-toned calling card. Underneath Holly's name she saw an address in a smaller font: Moore Lodge, 213 Irvington Street. Could this be *the* Moores of Moore Lumber? She'd read about them in the society section of the newspaper but had never met them. Violet had, however, experienced the squeeze of their reach when a representative from Moore Lumber had come out a few months before Roger had passed, all but demanding they sell the timber on their wooded property. Roger had refused, but the man had hounded them.

Of the mind that all people should be given the benefit of doubt, Violet kept her voice even and didn't reflect the distaste she felt at the company they stood for.

Miss Moore linked her arm through her uncle's. "I wish Matthew had been able to come with us." She turned to Violet, flashing two dimples. "He's my intended."

Violet tucked the card in the pocket of her broadcloth apron, trying her best to be congenial. "I see. How nice." She directed Miss Moore back to talk of flowers. "Did you have any color preferences, or would you like to go with the more traditional, white-wedding palette?"

Miss Moore disentangled herself from her uncle and leaned on the counter by the register, getting closer to Violet and saying in a conspiratorial fashion, "I like color and don't consider myself a person of tradition."

A faint scent of lavender and rose accompanied her nearness and words.

A low chuckle escaped Mr. Moore. "No, indeed not."

Uncle and niece shared a light laugh, and Violet couldn't help but like them. They were obviously a close family and one who shared a sense of humor.

"I like color myself," said Violet, "as you can well testify." She signaled with her arm around the shop at the bounty of colorful blooms and gift items within. Walking around the counter, Violet motioned for them to follow her. "Come this way. I want to show you my product books. It will give you an idea of what kind of flowers you can select." Violet led them to a little table and a few chairs under a bower of hanging plants: philodendrons, ivies, and ferns. Several books lay strewn atop the table. "Please take a seat," Violet told Mr. and Miss Moore. After they settled in their seats, Violet opened a green, cloth-bound book and flipped to the first page. She slid it toward Miss Moore. "Please, take a look."

Last year Violet had hired a local artist to paint watercolor images of the flowers she carried, and she had bound them into books for her customers to page through. It had been an expensive undertaking but well worth it.

Miss Moore looked for a few seconds at each page she turned. "My, there are so many beautiful kinds, and these are such lovely illustrations. I'm not sure what to select. What do you recommend?"

Mr. Moore pointed to an illustration of a pink English garden rose. "Your mother loved pale pink roses."

"Did she?" Miss Moore asked.

She smiled, but it reflected the sadness her uncle had displayed earlier. By their use of past tense, Violet assumed Miss Moore's mother was deceased.

Wanting to help them make the best choice, Violet said, "Ah, a Damask Perpetual variety named Jacques Cartier. It is most fragrant. Too cold to grow this rose here, but I can get them shipped in from a grower in Missouri."

Miss Moore looked up; her eyes widened. "You don't say? Does the pink rose have a certain meaning?"

With crisp blue eyes, as blue as forget-me-nots, Mr. Moore caught Violet's eyes as he spoke. "Gentleness and admiration, I believe."

"I'm surprised, sir. Are you versed in the language of flowers?" Violet asked.

Not that men didn't know that there were purposeful sentiments behind the giving of flowers, but most weren't interested in the details, only the application.

He focused on Violet, an unwavering gaze. "Oh, not really. I read it somewhere."

Violet thought well of a man who didn't back down. She held him in higher esteem because of it. That had been one of Roger's best attributes, but come to think of it, also his worst and likely what had led to his death.

Miss Moore lifted her eyes to Violet's. "You must know all about the flower meanings."

Not normally a blusher, Violet sensed a heat rushing to her cheeks. "I do. Many customers ask for my help in constructing a meaningful bouquet of flowers."

Miss Moore flipped through a few more of the thick watercolor pages, with a rustle. "What should I pair with the roses for a statement of love and devotion?"

Violet expounded on the choices. "The classic red rose, of course, is the best choice, but others are red tulips, peonies, chrysanthemums, carnations, and jasmine. Of these, and for a late June wedding, I would recommend peonies, carnations, and jasmine, and I should have those available locally."

"Then that's what we shall have," Mr. Moore said. "Along with the pink roses, in remembrance of your mother."

As it had a few minutes before, the same kind smile graced his face, a quite handsome one in Violet's estimation.

Miss Moore smiled first at Violet then turned to her uncle. "That sounds marvelous. Thank you, Uncle Devon."

He reached out and patted his niece on the hand. "You're welcome, my dear."

A sudden regret surfaced in Violet for not having children. She and Roger hadn't done anything to oppose that outcome, but no baby had ever resulted from what little intimacy they had shared.

It would have been lovely to have had a daughter. The thought rolled around in Violet's mind.

"It must be such fun to work in such a pleasant place, surrounded by flowers."

Miss Moore's statement shook Violet from her regrets.

She answered, "Most days." The words slipped out with honesty, surprising Violet. "Ah, I meant to say yes, but I do confess there are times I long for quiet, peaceful days at home."

What Violet didn't say was that she found the retail

aspect of the shop challenging. Not the business end but the public. It wore her out, being in a constant state of having to be pleasant and accommodating to everyone who waltzed through her shop door. Oh, not that she desired to be mean or grumpy. No, Violet just craved privacy sometimes, and she had little of that anymore. But perhaps taking on another hand to assist customers would ease her burden.

Mr. Moore hiked one thick but not bushy eyebrow skyward. "You must be terribly busy then."

Nodding, Violet said, "I am, and it's only me in the shop since…" She paused. She didn't want to spill her fairly recent grief out to a gentleman she had met only a few minutes ago. "Well, for a while."

She tucked her gaze down, back to the books on the table but glanced up when Miss Moore spoke.

"Are you seeking assistance?"

Her eyes sparkled, shimmering like Czech beads an indeterminate color of brownish hazel.

Wasn't I just praying for help this morning?

Had God sent His answer so soon?

"Well, yes. In fact, I had planned to put a help-wanted sign in the window today, but surely you wouldn't…"

Violet didn't get the rest of her words out.

Nodding, Miss Moore said, "I'd be most interested."

Mr. Moore objected for the first time. "But what will Matthew say?"

"Tish, tosh." Miss Moore flapped a graceful hand in

the air. "He won't mind, I'm sure."

"Still, talk it over with him," Mr. Moore said, his tone firm.

Not paying her uncle much heed, Miss Moore forged ahead and asked, "How many hours of help do you require?"

Violet could not mistake the eagerness in Miss Moore's tone, but was she ready to hire someone today? She had no idea of the young woman's skills or if she had any experience with hard work.

Running her gaze over Miss Moore again, Violet thoroughly doubted the woman would be up to the task, but she decided to give her the job description, regardless. "Maybe…three mornings a week."

Miss Moore tinkled out a light laugh. "I see you must be wondering about my aptitude. I worked as a maid and helped my aunt and uncle on their farm before…" She flicked her gaze to her uncle then back to Violet. "Well, less than a year ago."

Taken aback, Violet let slip, "I…see." But she did not. A significant change must have happened within the timeframe Miss Moore mentioned. By all appearances, Miss Moore was the picture of a well-off, young society lady, unaccustomed to labor of any kind. "And why would a soon-to-be-married, well-advantaged young woman want to be a shop girl? Forgive me my candor."

Violet believed in being straightforward.

"My niece can hold her own with a broom and a

dustbin. Do not worry on that account," Mr. Moore said, speaking as if he were proud of that fact.

Violet decided to make things clear to them. "Well, the job would mainly require one to be of service to the public, assisting with orders and the like. Some light cleaning as well and handling the flowers and plants." Violet thought a second. "Discuss the position with your fiancé, as your uncle urged. If he is in agreement, we can talk more."

A wide smile, exposing near perfect teeth, graced Miss Moore's face. "Wonderful! Thank you. I'll inform you of his thoughts as soon as I'm able."

Violet hated to let Miss Moore down, but she couldn't imagine a man giving his wife permission to work out of the home, unless it were a family business.

Mr. Moore pushed back from the table and rose. "We should get back, Holly. I have a meeting at noon."

He gave his niece a hand to help her up.

Violet stood along with her customers and said, as she walked them to the door, "I'm sure I'll be seeing you again soon. Thank you so much for stopping in and for your business. I look forward to creating something special for your wedding, Miss Moore."

Extending her hand, Violet shook Miss Moore's.

Miss Moore flashed another winning smile Violet's way. "It is I who should thank you for your expertise. I will inform you as soon as I can about my availability. Good day."

With a spring in her step, she walked out of the shop

door, which Mr. Moore held open.

Still leaning against the door, he caught Violet's gaze. "Forgive my saying so, but you seem the semblance of your namesake."

He cleared his throat and dropped his gaze a second, as if repenting of speaking.

Violet did see herself as reserved and holding a quiet beauty, of a kind, which the botanical violet was said to be known for. Roger had always said so.

She took Mr. Moore's words as a compliment—though Violet would rather have been perceived as something more exotic than the modest and humble violet—and replied simply, "Why, thank you."

He lifted his forget-me-not eyes again and tipped his head toward her. "Not at all." A reserved smile arched his lips. "Good day, Mrs. Brooks."

He turned and left, closing the door softly behind him, leaving a whiff of clove and bergamot behind him.

Through the glass panes of the front window, Violet watched niece and uncle amble away from the shop, arm in arm. Not one to form attachments easily, a slight sadness picked at Violet.

It would be nice to have the cheery company of Miss Moore in the shop, she decided, and she began to hope Miss Moore's fiancé would agree to their employment scheme.

Expelling a large breath, Violet turned and walked back to her worktable to finish the arrangement she'd been making before the Moores had walked into

Fragrant Sentiments, undeniably brightening her day. She whistled as she nestled carnations next to voluptuous branches of lilacs and pictured Mr. Moore's forget-me-not eyes.

I must have flowers,
always, always.

Claude Monet

CHAPTER TWO

Just a little more... Violet stretched out her arm and groaned. She gripped the top of the ladder with one hand and worked at hanging a paper banner on a nail with her other, but she hadn't positioned the ladder close enough.

"Oh, bother!" she growled out, as her foot slipped on the rung she stood on and the banner fluttered from her grasp.

"Here. Let me," a deep voice said, startling her.

Concentrating so hard, Violet hadn't heard anyone come into Fragrant Sentiments. She looked down from the five extra feet she stood at and spied Mr. Moore fishing for the looped string of the banner among the leaves of a Ficus tree.

He pulled it out. "Ah, ha!"

A warm smile lit up his face. A twinkle in his eye danced when he tipped his gaze up at Violet. Violet wobbled, as if she might slip again, but she gripped the ladder firmly with both hands.

"Thanks so much, but I think I need to move the ladder over a bit. My arm is too short," she told him before she backed down the ladder with care.

When she set her feet on the floor, she extended her hand for the end of the banner.

However, Mr. Moore held it fast. "No, no. You must allow me." And before Violet could protest, Mr. Moore shifted the ladder over and climbed up it, like a man half his age. He hung the end of the banner on the nail without incident. "There."

He sounded satisfied and came back down.

But instead of being grateful, annoyance simmered in her heart. Violet hadn't asked for his help, and she certainly didn't need it.

"Thanks," she squeaked out.

He looked up at the banner. "A big sale, huh?"

In stenciled letters, Violet had spelled out, "All flowers here 30% off," on the pennant-shaped flaps of the banner.

"I'm trying to get through some product before it expires."

He looked back at her, concern lowering his eyebrows. "Don't you have a cooler?"

"I do, but it's just a small, insulated room that I keep

blocks of ice in. The temperature of the space is difficult to control."

"I see." Mr. Moore smiled again, and Violet repented of her less than kind thoughts about him. "I was in Chicago not long ago and stopped at a flower shop that boasted an electric cooler."

Again, irritation rubbed at Violet, like an itchy collar. "I could never afford such a thing. It must be terribly expensive."

In truth, she and Roger had discussed investing in an electric air cooler to keep the flowers fresh, but in the end, they had both determined it to be too costly and too much of a risk.

"Yes. I suppose they must be." Mr. Moore's warm tone wavered, likely due to the starchy way Violet had responded to the mention of the cooler. He looked down at the tips of his shiny, brown shoes. "I don't mean to take up your time, Mrs. Brooks, but I told Holly I would get this to you."

With eyes full of unasked questions, he focused on Violet momentarily before pulling a small, handwritten notecard out of the inner pocket of his casual, taupe suit jacket. He held it out to her.

Taking the note from him, their fingers brushed, and Violet pulled back too quickly, sending the note to the floor. "Oh, dear. Nothing wants to stay within my clasp this morning."

Violet's hand fluttered to the hollow of her neck. *He must think I'm a clumsy lout.*

Mr. Moore stooped down and retrieved the note from the floor.

"I can't imagine why," he told her, placing it in her open palm with a light touch.

Violet's fingers folded around the thick, linen, cream-colored cardstock, a distinctive warmth kissing her wispy hairline at the back of her neck at his veiled compliment. "Thank you. Do give my regards to your niece."

He stood still, watching her for a few seconds, then continued. "Should I wait while you open it? In case you'd like to send a response?"

"Oh, certainly."

What is the matter with me? I need a second cup of tea.

Violet fumbled with the seal and opened the note, reading through it quickly, trying not to squirm under Mr. Moore's intent observation of her.

The note relayed that Miss Moore would be available to work immediately up to the week of her wedding and could start again the week following, if such was agreeable to Violet. Tucking the note back in the envelope, Violet wondered just who was hiring whom. Miss Moore seemed to have arranged things and assumed Violet would hire her, with few to no questions asked. Violet hadn't imagined finding anyone so swiftly, but she knew she needed help, and who better than sweet Miss Moore?

Clearing her throat, Violet said, "You may tell Miss Moore that I'll expect her first thing Monday morning.

Eight O'clock sharp. We'll discuss other details at that time."

Mr. Moore smiled, and Violet noticed how his eyes crinkled at the corners. The creases made him look even more distinguished.

"Holly will be so pleased," he replied. "She deserves to be happy."

"Don't we all?"

The question slipped out, a whispered thought, before Violet could take it back. Why did she so often speak without thinking first? It dismayed Violet. It was a habit she had not grown out of.

Mr. Moore tipped his head back and laughed. "Well, we'd all like to think so, wouldn't we?" Then he turned serious. "Now, I must go, but I'll leave my card with you."

With his middle and pointer finger, he plucked a business card out of the breast pocket of his jacket, as gracefully as a card shark, and arched his arm to give it to Violet.

She took it and forced herself to smile. "Thank you."

Mr. Moore tipped his hat. "I feel quite certain we'll be seeing more of each other, Mrs. Brooks."

He left before Violet could decide whether she agreed with him or not.

She threw up her hands in mild frustration and went to organize the flowers in buckets under the sale sign, but try as she might, Violet could not clear her mind of thoughts about Mr. Devon Moore.

After Violet had arranged the sale flowers to her satisfaction, she went to start on the orders she had for the day. Almost done with the first order, six yellow roses in a vase with greens, Violet glanced up when the door's bell clanged. A handsome, heavy-set woman, dressed smartly in navy blue and lavender, marched into the shop, holding a clear vase of flowers. She set it down with some force upon the counter.

"I specifically asked for something pretty."

Violet blinked in shock and took in the arrangement she had made yesterday. It looked the same to her, stylized and more simplistic than the usual full-blown, English-garden-style variety of arrangements. That word *pretty* had gotten Violet in more than one fix with an unhappy customer. Everyone had a different meaning for the word, and what was pretty to one customer might not be considered so by another.

Holding back the sigh she longed to spill out, Violet asked, "And what is it you find fault with, ma'am?"

The woman had no qualms about expelling a heave of air. "Well, anyone can see it's much too tall and thin. It should be more…full."

The woman flapped her hands in the air on either side of the vase.

"I am sorry this is not to your taste. Please excuse me while I check the order." Violet leafed through the orders from yesterday, still stacked by the register. She pulled out an order she recognized with the name Mrs. Woodford at the top. "Ah, I see you ordered a large-vase arrangement for your home in pastel shades. Is that correct?"

"Well, yes, but this is not what I wanted." Mrs. Woodford huffed and had the audacity to roll her prominent, brown eyes.

"And could you specify exactly what you would like?" Violet reminded herself that the customer was always right, but it rankled against her spirit, regardless.

Mrs. Woodford pointed to the arrangement Violet had finished minutes ago. "Like that one, there. In fact, I'll take that one."

Smiling with premature satisfaction, Mrs. Woodford nodded, wobbling several of the peach-colored, silk roses on her hat.

"I am sorry, but it's not for sale."

Mrs. Woodford narrowed her eyes. "Excuse me? You are selling flowers here in your shop, are you not?"

Violet counted under breath, using the numeric scale to calm her nerves. "You misunderstand me. This arrangement is for a special order for a funeral."

"I see." Mrs. Woodford's words came out less snide, but she still looked put-out to Violet.

An ache started to throb in Violet's jaw from her clenching her teeth. She focused on trying to relax.

"However, I could make something similar for you. Would that be to your satisfaction?" she asked her customer.

Shrugging her well-padded shoulders, Mrs. Woodford said, "I suppose that will have to suffice."

Really, would it hurt some people to be more gracious?

"Will you be waiting for the arrangement, or do you want it delivered?"

Mrs. Woodford sniffed and lifted her nose in the air. "Hmm, I'm certainly not going to be carrying a large arrangement five blocks back to my home, now, am I?"

"Delivery then?" Violet double checked, losing patience by the second.

"That *is* what I said."

God grant me patience, Violet silently prayed, but she said, "I'll have that to you tomorrow by early afternoon."

"Hmm, I suppose that'll do."

There was no pleasing the woman, it seemed.

"Same address as before?" Violet asked.

"That's right. My husband and I live next to the Moores. Such comings and goings on there of late— ever since Devon Moore came back."

"Back from where?" Violet couldn't help asking.

She searched Mrs. Woodford's prominent eyes for what she hoped would be the truth.

"You don't know?" Mrs. Woodford leaned toward Violet over the counter dividing the workstation from the retail floor, her hefty bosom smooshing the stems of several hyacinths Violet had laid on the counter. "Moore Lodge has sat nearly empty for ten years."

Violet vaguely recalled some gossip she'd heard some years back about the Moores, but she couldn't recall what it had been about. She did remember

Grapevine Lodge having that unlived-in look, from the few times she'd had occasion to drive by that way.

"And what made Mr. Moore return after such a lengthy period?" Violet asked.

"No one really knows. He had been overseeing Moore Lumber up north somewhere, but lumbering has been declining some. Perhaps that's why he came back. Mr. Moore almost sold Moore Lumber and the lodge last December, but that fell through."

Her interest piqued, Violet had to ask, "Why?"

"His niece, of course."

That meant nothing to Violet. What would Holly have done to interrupt his plans? "I don't think I quite understand."

Mrs. Woodford leaned back, standing up straight. "Apparently, they both had thought each other dead."

She pulled out a hankie and dabbed at her perspiring forehead, though it felt temperate in the shop to Violet.

No wonder Mr. Moore dotes on his niece. Violet could hardly imagine the circumstances of such a strange occurrence.

"That's old news. However, I hear tell there's to be a wedding soon."

Pinning Violet with wide, prying eyes, Mrs. Woodford clearly fished for confirmation and details.

"I really couldn't say."

It wasn't a lie. Violet couldn't say, and it wasn't her place to.

"Hmm, well, Moore Lumber has merged with

Peterson Lumber Company. Perhaps Mr. Moore is marrying his niece off to the owner's son to further solidify the merger; I wager."

Listening to gossip never failed to turn Violet's stomach. "I'm sure I wouldn't know." She gathered the flowers she had splayed out on the table, awaiting a fresh cut and placement in a short, round vase. "Now, if you'll excuse me, Mrs. Woodford, I have much work to do, including your replacement arrangement. Have a pleasant afternoon."

Turning at an angle to Mrs. Woodford, without fully turning her back, Violet began arranging flowers in a clear, glass vase, half full of water.

Mrs. Woodford turned and glanced back. "Hmm, well, mind it's full and pretty this time."

Violet cringed at the use of that distasteful, overused, generic word. "Of course."

She gave Mrs. Woodford a tight flash of a smile.

"A good day to you." Finally, Mrs. Woodford turned and exited the shop.

Violet heaved a sigh of relief. As she created an arrangement for the hotel downtown, she mulled over what Mrs. Woodford had said about the Moores, who sounded like a family with secrets. She supposed everyone had secrets; Violet knew she did. But still she wondered just who Devon Moore was and what had kept him from his home for ten years.

For I shall learn from leaf and flower,
that color every drop they hold,
to change the lifeless wine of grief,
to living gold.

– Sara Teasdale

CHAPTER THREE

It's one thing, seeing someone I know intimately that has passed, but encountering the dead body of a simple acquaintance or a stranger...

Violet shivered and forced herself to walk into the dim funeral parlor, where Mr. Manchett had told her to place the arrangements. Gulping down a lump in her throat, Violet girded herself with determination and walked on. She had to admit that this part of being a florist had not gotten any easier.

The moss-green, carpeted floor squeaked beneath her feet, though she treaded lightly. Gas sconces on opposite walls shed some light but left the chairs in the middle of the room cloaked in shadow. The smell of old roses, lemon furniture polish, and the hint of some chemical scent weighed down the air, along with the stuffiness of a home after a long winter in need of a good airing and spring cleaning.

Since she could remember, Violet had hated seeing any dead creatures. She held her brothers responsible for her abhorrence of all things macabre. They had tormented her weekly with a steady round of dead insects, amphibians, and small rodents, planted between the sheets of her bed, until she'd complained to her mother, who had not believed her at first but then, thankfully, had caught the two criminals in the act.

Of their own accord, Violet's feet slowed as she neared the stands, positioned on either side of an open, wooden casket with what looked like pale, pink silk lining on the interior. Violet set the vase of flowers she carried on one stand and averted her eyes from the slight human form she glimpsed, in her peripheral vision, nestled snugly within its resting place. She repositioned several flowers that had been jostled out of place before turning to go retrieve the last arrangement waiting on the floral cart Webster had pushed a few blocks to the funeral home from Fragrant Sentiments.

But as Violet pivoted on her heel, a voice shattered the quiet. "Violet?"

Violet reacted with a scream, sudden and near ear-splitting.

"Wow! You still have strong lungs." A laugh followed the words.

Trying to calm her hammering heart, Violet sucked in a breath and squinted at the corner of the room where the voice had come from. She took in a man, who appeared to be in his forties with a nondescript, charcoal-gray suit and a balding head with dark hair. Her breathing slowed as he stood and came closer.

Violet studied him and something familiar about the cut of his jaw and the slightly crooked nose flashed through her mind. "Fr...ankie?" She struggled to get the name out. "Frankie Dermot?"

He winked, a quick flash of his right eye. "What gave it away? My dashing good looks?"

Violet fluttered her eyelashes. "It's rather a shock to see you. It's been...how long?"

Frankie smiled. "Near fifteen years, I'd reckon."

The feelings Violet had once held for the rapscallion of her youth—her first love—rushed back.

"Why...are you here?" she choked out, placing a shaking hand over her heart.

He shrugged one shoulder. "Stella was my niece, as you might remember. I came back to help my sister navigate through this time. Her husband passed last year, so it's been a heavy load on her."

"Oh, yes. I recall Mr. Shelton passing." Violet paused then spilled out, "My husband died around that same time."

A vise-like pinch tightened around Violet's rib cage

as she thought of how Roger had died. The more she thought about it, the more she was sure the representative from Moore Lumber had set the trap.

Frankie reached out and touched her elbow. "I'm so sorry. I heard about the accident, of course, but I was out West, covering a story, and couldn't come to the services."

Violet nodded. "Yes. Thank you." She took a deep breath and looked into those blue-grey eyes she had once been so fond of. "Things must be going well for you, writing for *The Chicago Daily News*."

"You heard?"

Violet smiled at his surprise. "Your mother mentioned it in passing to me not long ago at church."

"Yes, I enjoy being a reporter." Frankie smiled wider then looked toward the casket, where his niece Stella lay. "Look, let me escort you outside, and we can finish our conversation away from…" he paused and frowned, his mouth, eyes, and eyebrows all drooping, "this sadness."

Violet took his offered arm and allowed herself to be led outside. When they exited the funeral home into the fresh air, she remembered she still had work to do. "Oh, but I have another vase to place. I should…"

With a certain calmness, Frankie captured the hand that she used to point back to the funeral home. "Do not fret. I'll take it in for you in a minute."

She didn't pull away from the warmth of his large hand.

He swung her hand and arm out before letting go. "First, let me look at you. One can hardly see anything in the shadows of the interior of Matchetts'."

Despite the slight impropriety, Violet laughed. "Agreed."

His gaze swept Violet from her silk-flower-embellished, straw hat to the sturdy shoes on her feet. "You hardly look a day older."

Violet sensed a flush coming and chided herself. *What? Am I sixteen again?*

"You're too kind," she said aloud.

Examining Frankie, Violet couldn't quite say the same. His hair had thinned, a slight paunch thickened his middle, and deep creases at the corners of his eyes and at the top of his cheekbones all spoke of the passage of time. However, the twinkle in his bright eyes and his deep, smooth voice remained unchanged.

He cocked his head, setting his eyes on Violet's. "Now, tell me about your flower shop. Mother said you recently opened it."

A warmth spread in Violet's heart at his interest. "It has been a dream come true for me, and it was a big step for Roger and me, coming from selling our plants and a few cut flowers at our home in the country. Roger loved the shop, and I miss working with him."

Violet looked down and sniffed before continuing. Frankie gave her time and kept quiet.

She tilted her face up and met Frankie's eyes. "Anger overtakes me sometimes when I dwell on the fact that

Roger is gone and not able to live out this dream with me."

"You were very close then?" he asked.

Violet couldn't mistake the hint of disappointment she heard sandwiched between his slower, softer words. "We were, and, of course, I do miss him, but it's the injustice of it that fuels my angst."

Frankie shook his head slowly and sighed. "The more I travel and write, the more I'm finding out how much injustice the world contains."

Instead of the playful twinkle, a soulfulness in his eyes connected Frankie to Violet.

He understands. Violet had a sudden urge to spill all the details about Roger's death she'd built up in her mind, over the lumber company's involvement and supposed responsibility, but she bit her tongue, being a naturally cautious person.

On the verge of saying more, she was interrupted, several carriages pulling into the funeral home's lot. "I really must get the other arrangement."

"Let me."

Frankie followed her to the floral cart. Once Violet had plucked the vase out of the cart, he took it from her.

"Thank you. And again, I'm sorry about your niece." Violet hoped Frankie heard the sincerity in her words.

"Thanks. I'll tell Mother. Will you be coming to the service?" he asked.

Violet shook her head. "No. I'm sorry. I have too much to do in the shop before my new employee starts on Monday."

His eyes, hopeful and bright, sought an answer in hers. "Could we…perhaps, meet for coffee or lunch before I return to Chicago?"

Without mulling it over, Violet agreed. "That would be nice. I'll look forward to it."

Surprising herself, the truth of Violet's words lifted her spirits.

He grinned, his lips closed, spreading into his cheeks. "I'll call on you soon."

Turning, Violet watched him as he took long strides toward the funeral home. Before entering he looked back at her and waved. She returned the hand motion and began to push the floral cart back to the shop, thinking all the way how odd it was that in a matter of two days she had met and been drawn to both Mr. Devon Moore and her old schoolmate, the first man to catch her eye, Frankie Dermot. And for a few seconds Violet entertained thoughts of remarriage. But she promptly reined in her thoughts to more practical matters, like how she was going to afford to pay Miss Moore, and on top of that, how she could get the information she sought through the link she now had to the Moore family. In Violet's mind, this brought her one step closer to achieving her vow.

Roses are red,
violets are blue,
I'll never love someone
the way I love you.

~

Anonymous

CHAPTER FOUR

Violet unhinged the sandwich board, opening and standing it up on the sidewalk in front of Fragrant Sentiments. She'd taken a few minutes before opening the shop to write in chalk on the board about the details of the sale she had running. She stood up straight and inhaled slowly, her eyes rolling shut a moment as she took in the smells and sounds around her. As much as Violet adored rural life, there were some positive things to be said about being in town.

These early morning hours before the rush of shoppers flooded the day met a need for something in her that Violet couldn't name. A sense of quiet in which to offer up a prayer and blessing on the day anchored her. The cooler temperatures before the sun hit its zenith awakened her, and the thought that she belonged with the other business owners in town made the mornings her favorite part of the day.

Violet sniffed and listened. The delightful aroma of fresh-baked cinnamon buns wafted on the breeze from the direction of the bakery. Mrs. Miller's broom scratched the stoop in front of the mercantile with a scritch-scratch, while Mr. Miller unrolled the storefront's awning, the roller's wheels squeaking, calling out for a dab of grease.

"Mrs. Brooks?"

Flashing her eyes open, Violet faced Miss Holly Moore, dressed in a sedate, stone-gray shirtwaist and skirt.

By force of habit, Violet brushed her hands down the front of her apron. "Good morning. You…caught me off guard. It's my custom to admire the early mornings for a few minutes before opening up shop."

Violet did not want to appear flustered in front of Miss Moore.

Miss Moore flashed a toothy smile, and Violet couldn't help but feel drawn to the young woman even more. "A wonderful practice. My Aunt Nel likes to greet the day with a cup of tea and her Bible. She's fond of telling me that there's not a problem too large that can't be hemmed in by those two things."

Violet opened the shop door and motioned for Holly to enter. "Your aunt sounds like a wise lady."

"That she is," Miss Moore agreed.

"Is she your Uncle Devon's sister?" Violet asked, as she followed Holly into the shop.

"Oh, no. My mother's."

"Ah, I see."

Violet desired to ask more about the family, but she led Miss Moore to the counter and got started filling her in on the basic jobs she would be responsible for.

When Violet finished the round of instructions, Miss Moore spoke up. "My, that's a lot to remember."

Pinched brows and a quiet response told Violet that Miss Moore worried about what was expected of her.

"You'll catch on in no time. Any questions, just ask."

Violet tried to ease her new employee's mind as she filled the till with an assortment of bills and coins from the money bag which she had taken out of the safe and stashed under the counter shortly before Miss Moore had arrived.

The bell jingled as the shop door opened.

"Our first customer." Violet smiled and motioned Miss Moore forward. "You can listen and assist, if need be." She plucked a green apron off the nearby rack on the wall. "Your armor."

Violet passed it to Miss Moore.

"Thank you."

Miss Moore took it, grinned, and donned her apron, wrapping the ties around and fastening it with a bow in the front in the middle of her waist.

Nodding, she walked with Violet to meet the man who had entered. After exchanging pleasantries with her customer, Violet discerned a divided heart in him as he deliberated between selecting several different kinds of flowers to purchase. A whiff of deception seemed to filter from him, and with uncanny intuition Violet perceived him as a foxglove, a flower both beautiful and enchanting but touched by mystery and insincerity.

The man pulled a white handkerchief from the inner breast pocket of his cream-colored, linen suit coat and mopped his perspiring forehead. "Yes, yes…I'll go with the six roses. Pink and red, if you please."

"Certainly. I'll get that wrapped up for you." Violet made to move toward the cool room, but the man stopped her.

"Ah, wait. I…I best get two different assortments. Twelve roses total. Six in one and six in the other."

Violet hiked one eyebrow up. "Both red and pink?"

Grimacing as if in pain, the man dripped with uncertainty, his narrow eyes squinting more so. "I…I'm not sure. Perhaps the same." He deliberated a moment, tapping his index finger on his chin. "Yes, exactly the same." He smiled and nodded then changed his mind and flapped his hand in the air. "No, no. Best do one bouquet all red."

Violet prayed for patience, not one of her better virtues.

"As you wish," she told her customer, then motioned

to Miss Moore, who followed her to the cool room.

They gathered up the roses and some greenery and brought them to the wrapping counter, where a huge roll of brown paper on a metal stand with a saw-toothed edge stood waiting. Violet unrolled and ripped off a section of paper.

Demonstrating how to layer the flowers and greens to make a pleasing ensemble, Violet pulled a tail of red ribbon on a spool, giving the end to Miss Moore. "Please cut this and tie up the wrap, and then you can do the next one from start to finish."

Miss Moore nodded and accomplished the task with only one reminder from Violet.

"Good! Thank you." Violet sent Holly a sweet smile, thankful she had a helper. "Let's go ring these up."

Holly kept time with Violet's stride but whispered, "Why do you suppose he needs two bouquets?"

Violet had her guesses but didn't want to put a damper on Miss Moore's first day by speculating on someone else's possible improprieties.

"I'm not certain," she replied. "Here you are, sir."

Violet held out the wrapped bouquet to the man, and Holly did likewise.

The man swallowed, his Adam's apple bobbing. "I've changed my mind."

Not again!

"What is it?" Violet asked.

"I'd like these delivered, instead."

Violet gritted her teeth but took down the details for

delivery. "Very well. Card messages?"

The man narrowed his eyes at her, like Violet had asked something terrible.

"I'll write them," he grouched out and made a come-hither motion with his fingers.

Violet selected two small cards and envelopes for him, passing them his way. He snatched them from Violet's hand, plucked up the feather quill pen by the register, and started scratching away. Turning her back, Violet left him to his task.

"Webster will be here at noon to run deliveries. We don't accept delivery orders for after noon, unless it's something special," she explained to Miss Moore.

The bell jingled again, and Violet spied a middle-aged woman entering the shop. "I'm going to help the woman who just walked in. Would you finish with this gentleman and tie his messages on the bouquets when he's done?"

"Of course." All eager to please, Miss Moore grinned and marched to do as Violet instructed.

Violet asked how she could be of service to the woman, who effused an atmosphere of cheer. A little too cheerful for Violet, perhaps, but the world needed more people like this woman, who reminded Violet of the lovely lilac, brightening all with its perfume, though fading a bit too fast. She helped the woman select flowers for a birthday bouquet and wrapped them up for her.

"Oh, drat!" Miss Moore exclaimed as she bent to

pick up something off the floor that she had dropped. She rose, holding two envelopes and two enclosure cards, placing them on the wrapping counter. "I'm not sure which message goes with which envelope."

A row of faint lines etched Miss Moore's normally smooth brow.

"Weren't the envelopes sealed with the pot of heated wax I keep by the register?" Violet asked.

Shaking her head, Miss Moore admitted, "He forgot to seal them after he finished."

"Could you read them and tell the difference?" Violet asked, tying a yellow ribbon around the bouquet of yellow tulips and blue hyacinths, a blend conveying friendship and sincerity—perfect for the birthday of a good friend.

Holly twisted her hands together. "Oh, I don't know. Mr. Clemons was most particular. I feel like I would be intruding on his private affairs."

Miss Moore's cheeks flushed pink.

Violet sighed. "I'll take a look. Let me finish ringing this lady up."

The idea in hiring Holly had been to take some tasks off Violet's proverbial plate, not add to them. Violet calmed her blooming annoyance with legitimate rationalizations. *It's her first day. She's probably nervous, and everything is new.*

Finishing with the cheerful woman, Violet hurried back to Miss Moore.

She held out her hand. "Let's see."

With a sheepish flash of her dark eyes, Miss Moore placed the messages in Violet's hand. Since Cheerful Woman had left and no one was in the shop, Violet read them aloud.

"Darling, allow me to express my admiration and desire to be at your side. I'm hoping these flowers suffice until I can see you again, your Stanley Bear."

Her lip curled up on reflex, and Violet glanced at Miss Moore's wide eyes. They both started giggling at the same time.

"Stanley Bear?" Miss Moore repeated and giggled again.

Violet rolled her eyes. "That's nothing. You should hear what silly endearments people sign with sometimes." She picked up the other message and read it. "Happy Anniversary, Love Stanley."

Violet and Miss Moore shared a long, confused look.

"Oh, dear," Violet uttered, turning to study the addresses on the envelopes. One was in a wealthier portion of town, the other in a spot with more modest homes. "It's my guess that the mixed pink and red roses are for his wife, as they signify a longtime love. Regrettably, the six red roses mean a desire to be attached, an ardency, and are likely for a woman 'Stanley Bear' wishes to be…better acquainted with."

Miss Moore gasped and covered her mouth with her palm. "That's horrible."

"Yes, it is."

Violet thanked God that Robert had been a faithful man, God Fearing and not prone to indulge the flesh, but then Roger had often seemed to have more interest in flowers than in Violet. Oh, she knew Roger had cared for her deeply, but Violet had felt a fire lacking in their intimacy and, though unseemly for a woman to admit, she had on occasion wanted more.

Violet handed the card message she thought was for the wife to Miss Moore. "Here."

They tucked each message in its respective envelope and this time sealed them. Miss Moore finished tying the messages on the ribbons around the bouquets. Violet told her to stand them upright in a tin bucket in the cool room until Webster came to do the deliveries.

After Miss Moore completed that, Violet set her to stripping leaves off the lower portion of the stems of the roses that had come in that morning, using a knife, while Violet worked on one more arrangement that needed to be made for pickup in the afternoon.

A kind of happiness brightened Violet's heart as she quietly created, in the space she had come to cherish. With quick hands and flashes of her knife, Violet cut and arranged a mixed spring bouquet in a green, matte, glazed vase. Not thinking too intently about the design, Violet took in her shop with a smile on her face.

Rows of shining, colored and clear vases, perching on shelves in an open wardrobe, winked at her across the room. Sachets of scent and small bars of soap shaped like flowers occupied a dresser top nearby, while colorful scarves spilled out of the dresser's drawers. In the middle of the room an old pushcart contained a lush assortment of green and blooming plants.

Greeting cards lined a portion of one wall on narrow shelving Roger had constructed and put up. Some silk-flower arrangements in various pots adorned a round tabletop in the far corner of the room, and tiny, linen bags of hand-blended, floral teas lined a basket on an old dining chair, positioned near the counter.

Over the last few months, Violet had tucked more merchandise into the nooks and crannies of Fragrant Sentiments, until the shop had become a pleasing blend of gift items, potted plants, and fresh flowers, and she felt a glow of pride and contentment at her labors.

Webster came and left with deliveries. Miss Moore finished the roses, and Violet set her to the task of pricing some new gift items, while she delved into some paperwork. Before she knew it, Violet checked her watch, pinned to her breast, and saw the time approached to close the shop for lunch. Just as she was about to rise from her desk chair to inform Miss Moore, the bell jingled on the shop door. Violet's small corner office sat open to the shop except for what division an oriental screen allowed. She glanced up at the door and saw a poshly dressed gentleman in a light tan, pinstripe suit enter the room. He lifted his head, and even from across the room, the blue of Mr. Moore's eyes shimmered at Violet.

Filing away her normal reserve, Violet moved away

from her desk toward him, not knowing what she would say to him when she arrived at his side. But she didn't have to think about it too long, for Violet suddenly heard a squeal and a rush of skirts, as Miss Moore hurried to intercept her uncle.

They greeted each other, and Miss Moore began babbling away about the events of the morning, thankfully leaving out the mixed-up card messages.

Mr. Moore tipped his head back and laughed.

"A good start then?" he asked his niece.

A wide smile lifted Miss Moore's round cheeks. "Oh, yes. It was most educational and fun."

Violet had not equated the word "fun" with Fragrant Sentiments before, but thought Miss Moore's expression apt.

"I'm glad to hear you enjoyed yourself and that I didn't work you too hard," Violet said, joining Miss Moore and her uncle by the door.

The corners of Mr. Moore's eyes crinkled. "If you had, I'm sure Holly would have done well, regardless." He addressed his niece. "Ready to go home? I promised Matthew I'd escort you."

Miss Moore's voice dipped, and a waver in her tone accompanied her question. "Will he be late again?"

"A bit but not to worry. Gather your things." He glanced into Violet's eyes. "That is if you're ready to release Holly for the day?"

Violet nodded. "Why, yes. That's what we agreed upon." She turned to Miss Moore. "Thank you for your help this morning, Miss Moore."

"You're most welcome, but I do wish you'd call me Holly," Holly said.

"As you wish." Violet dipped her head. "Have a good afternoon, Holly."

"I'll see you tomorrow, Mrs. Brooks."

Violet smiled. "I should return the favor and insist you call me Violet."

An informal working atmosphere suited Violet much more than hearing an employee constantly calling her Mrs. Brooks all day. She'd rather be known simply as Violet.

Holly grinned. "Thank you, Violet."

She grabbed her bag and took her uncle's arm. Violet noticed that Holly must have already taken her apron off and hung it on the peg by the workstation.

"See you tomorrow," Violet said and fluttered her hand in a brief wave.

Holly waved back, then uncle and niece turned and made their way out. Mr. Moore threw back a glimmer of his blue eyes at Violet before they slipped away.

Violet stood by the door, watching them through the front window, and she recognized a definite hollow existed in the lack of Holly's presence in the shop. But more than that. Disappointment settled in Violet over the normal, polite exchange between herself and Mr. Moore. She had hoped for something else, but what that amounted to, she couldn't articulate.

Really! It was just yesterday you were entertaining

romantic thoughts about Frankie. Violet chided herself. Had she reverted to a swooning young woman in a matter of days?

Violet sighed, pulled the shade on the door's window down, fished her key out of her pocket, and inserted it in the keyhole, locking the door with a metallic click. She dallied back through the shop, on her way to eat lunch at her desk, her steps leaving a slight, empty echo behind her.

Stars will blossom in the darkness,
violets bloom beneath the snow.

Julia C.R. Dorr

CHAPTER FIVE

Holly held out a small envelope to Violet. "I found this on the floor, by the door when I came in this morning. I tucked it in my apron pocket and forgot to give it to you, with the rush of customers we had this morning."

Gazing at Holly, Violet could read the apology in her slightly upturned lips and wide-open eyes. Violet took the envelope. The writing on the front read: *To the sweetest Violet in the bunch.*

Talk about silly endearments.

Violet nodded and palmed the envelope against her skirt, avoiding meeting Holly's eyes. "Thank you."

Surely, Holly read the words on the envelope. What she must think!

Affixing her hat on her head with a pearl-tipped hat

pin, Violet tucked aside her embarrassment and lifted her eyes to Holly's. "I'll just be a half hour. Take messages if you need to. Are you sure you'll be fine on your own?"

Frankie had called and set a date with Violet to meet for that cup of coffee and lunch they'd talked about, and she was late. She had her qualms about leaving Holly alone, but Holly had proven herself a smart and reliable employee in the week she had worked at Fragrant Sentiments.

With all seriousness, Holly tipped her chin up, her cute but pointy nose elevated. "Oh, yes. I'll manage."

Violet smiled and caught up her bag. "Very well. I'll be back shortly."

She left, the door clanging behind her. After she walked a few feet from the shop and away from Holly's questioning eyes, Violet stopped on the sidewalk and pulled the envelope out. She studied it, sliding her fingers over the thick paper.

Expensive paper with flower petals pressed into the sheet. She brought it to her nose; it smelled vaguely of allspice. Despite it being five minutes after when she'd said she'd meet Frankie for lunch at The Northwesterner, Violet opened the message, sealed with red wax, impressed with the image of a rose. She unfolded the paper and exposed a dried pansy head. Picking up the pansy, she read the words written on the inside of the paper envelope.

You occupy my thoughts. I see you in my mind's eye in the morning when I rise and remember you before I fall asleep. I dare to not simply admire you in my heart but confess my fondness for you, sweet Violet. Your admirer.

Violet sucked in a breath and almost let the paper and flower fall from her grasp. She caught them as they slipped and folded the flower and message back up, safely stowing them in her bag before hustling to the hotel.

Really, who can it be?

Violet knew of no men who'd expressed any interest in romantic notions toward her. Yes, of late, she had exchanged pleasantries with Mr. Moore, and Frankie, but surely neither of them could be so smitten as to write her a love note. *Of all things!*

Violet tried to push thoughts of the note and her secret admirer from her mind, as she entered the hotel and found the dining room. The smell of toasted bread and roasted meat set her stomach to growling.

She spied Frankie at a bistro table for two among the busy lunch crowd.

"I'm so sorry," Violet gushed, arriving at his table.

Frankie smiled and jerked up from his seat. "Allow me."

He moved around the table and pulled out the empty chair for Violet.

She smiled back, not sure what to think of this chivalrous action in her old school chum. "Why, thank you."

Violet sat and Frankie helped her scoot the chair closer.

"How has your morning gone?" he asked, resuming his seat.

"Busy. Another funeral. Then various folks came in seeking flowers and gifts for an anniversary, two birthdays, and a new birth to celebrate."

Violet exhaled with a puff. She felt out of breath. She mentioned nothing about the surprise of the morning—the love note.

Frankie grinned, revealing that he still had a nice set of teeth. "Business is booming, then?"

"Well, I wouldn't say that. The good Lord has seen fit to bless my endeavors, thus far, but I do wonder how I can keep on with so few staff. I have hired a sweet young woman, and she is doing well, but between you and me, I can't afford to hire more help."

Finishing smoothing back a stray strand of hair from the back of her head that kept tickling her neck, Violet picked up the paper menu in front of her, glancing over it.

Frankie took notice of his menu as well. "That puts you in a tough spot. Hopefully, soon, profits will get you where you need to be."

Violet only nodded in response and didn't further the topic. She hadn't come to talk about business.

"I've heard the soup and toasted sandwich special is good," she told Frankie.

"Yes, that sounds tempting. I enjoy a good ham and cheese." Frankie lifted his eyes and focused on Violet. The light in his eyes appeared to dim, and his lips pressed into a thin line. "I know I mentioned this when I saw you last, but again, I am truly sorry about Roger. You didn't deserve his loss so soon after starting your dream."

Violet didn't want to look at the pity she discerned in his eyes and tipped her gaze back to her menu. For some reason today, she missed Roger afresh. Maybe because their anniversary hovered, in only a couple days' time. Violet sniffed and willed away the tears she could taste.

She forced herself to look up at Frankie. "I appreciate that. We would have celebrated twelve years together the day after tomorrow."

"Sorry," Frankie said again.

A few seconds of silence rested between them, and the drone of other people nearby, dining and visiting, filled in the space.

Ask him.

A prodding in her spirit opened Violet's mouth. "Actually, I meant to ask before, but I wonder if you'd be open to investigating and…writing a story on the Moore Lumber Company."

He perked up, a journalist at heart, always seeking the next good story. That's what Violet counted on, anyway.

"Oh? About?" Frankie asked.

Violet opened her mouth but didn't reply because a waitress came, filled their water glasses, and took their orders.

When she left, Violet revealed the core of her mission. "To expose their threats against Roger, me, our business, and possibly…even their involvement in… murder."

She paused, waiting for Frankie to protest or be shocked, but he puckered his lips in and out, listening.

"Go on," he told her.

Violet took a deep breath. "It started with badgering, a few months before Roger died. A representative of the company harassed us when we refused to sell the trees on our wooded property to the company. Our neighbors, the Greens, suffered the same treatment. Roger protested to management, but nothing ever came of it.

"One day Roger caught a lumberman, who said he was from the company, surveying our woods with his team. Roger chased him off, but he came back again. We were about to involve the police when Roger had his *accident*."

Frankie took a drink of water but kept his eyes trained on Violet. "And exactly what happened? How did he die?"

"He got his foot and leg caught in a steel trap." Violet looked down at her lap and brushed the plush velvet of her blue bag with a fingertip. "The doctor told me he lost a lot of blood, but he might have recovered if infection hadn't settled in." With her head still slightly bowed, Violet flicked her gaze up to Frankie's gray-blue eyes, trying to decipher his thoughts. She wanted to be clear. "Roger never set animal traps on our property, nor did our neighbors. The only other people who had been out in that area of the woods were the lumberman and his team."

Frankie grimaced and cocked his head to the left. "Any involvement by Moore Lumber would be very hard to prove." He snapped his fingers out of the blue and made Violet jump in her seat. "Come to think of it, Mom said Moore sold a portion of the company. It's now the Moore and Peterson Lumber Company."

Peterson? Isn't that the last name of Holly's fiancé? But then, there were quite a few folks carrying that surname.

"Interesting," Violet said. "Your point?"

"Dual ownership will make it even more difficult to attribute guilt to the company."

Violet let her bottom lip droop. "Oh."

That was disappointing.

Frankie uttered a light laugh. "But have no worries, I have a way of getting answers and uncovering the truth."

He smiled, making his face look fuller. His eyes warmed.

Violet worked hard to restrain the twinge of glee in her heart. "You will look into it for me, then?"

"Surely. It's the least I can do for an old friend."

His steady reply gave her hope; she was glad of someone with some clout being on her side.

But concern made Violet ask, "Are you sure it won't inconvenience or trouble your plans?"

He shook his head. "No. Mom asked me to stay an extra week or two, and I told her that I would." With a wide, foolish grin, Frankie continued, "Besides, if I get to see more of you and pursue a story, that's a win-win." He lifted his arms and palms up. "What better way to spend a week?" He lowered his arms and wrapped one hand around his water glass again, lifting it in a salute. "To old friends and making new memories."

He hiked his eyebrows up for a second, leaving Violet guessing as to why.

Could he be hinting at more than friendship? For less than a second, Violet let her mind suppose Frankie was her admirer, but she couldn't see him playing such a hidden role. Frankie had always liked to make a statement, a splash in the proverbial pool of life. He'd be bold, not hanging in the shadow of an anonymous love note. Unless he had changed.

Violet cleared her throat, picked up her glass, and raised it, though not as high as Frankie had. Her sense of decorum told her the water could be taken for wine, and people might think the flower shop owner indulged herself in the middle of the day.

"Agreed." She offered a modest smile and took a sip of water.

The waitress came back with their food, and the next few minutes were used up with eating and commenting on the meal.

Then Frankie asked, "So, do you have any names of people for me to investigate, beside Mr. Moore?"

He took a large bite of sandwich and chewed, his attention on Violet.

Violet shrugged. "The agent that threatened us never gave a name. He just said he represented the lumber company. We should have asked, I suppose. And maybe Roger knew, but he never told me."

"And why now? Why didn't you try to bring this story to light right after Roger died?"

Violet shook her head. "It was too soon, the grief too fresh. I didn't really think it all through until afterwards. At first, I saw it as an accident, but the more I've mulled it over, the more something doesn't add up."

After wiping his mouth on the dark green napkin, Frankie told her, "I'll make some discreet inquiries at Moore Lumber. I mean, Moore and Peterson Lumber Company, and see if I can dig up a name, and I'll go from there." He touched the side of his mouth and skewed his eyes up to the ceiling for a few moments, before swinging them back to Violet. "It could be the clerk or owner of the local dry goods store might recall who bought a steel trap. Of course, it could have been one they owned, stole, or borrowed. We'll see. I'll check all the leads I can."

Frankie stood, deposited more than enough money on the table to cover the bill and tip, and came around the table. He helped Violet up. Somehow, her hand found its way into his grasp.

His eyes penetrated Violet's. "And we can meet for

lunch in a few days and go over what I've discovered."

Frankie had dropped his nonchalant air and looked at her with purpose and intent, as if she were the one being investigated.

Violet wriggled her hand from his. "Thank you. Let's do that." Fighting a sudden urge to bolt from the room, Violet took a breath and counted her blessings. Frankie was willing to assist her. "I really am most grateful to you."

"I'm happy to help."

Frankie slipped back into his happy-go-lucky self and offered Violet his elbow. She took it, and he escorted her out of the dining room. Her gaze on the floor and her thoughts elsewhere, Violet nearly bumped into someone.

"Pardon me, Mrs. Brooks."

Whipping her head up, Violet's heart thumped in her ears, and her stomach plummeted when she realized Mr. Moore stood inches from her.

"Mr. Moore! I'm so sorry," Violet apologized, flustered yet again in his presence, much to her annoyance.

She squeezed Frankie's arm for support.

Mr. Moore transferred his gaze to Frankie. "I don't believe I've had the pleasure."

He extended his hand to Frankie in a friendly manner, but Violet spied an almost imperceptible flinch of the muscles by one of his eyes, telling her that Mr. Moore had more on his mind than a simple introduction.

Frankie shook Mr. Moore's hand. "Franklin Dermot, an old friend of Violet's."

The handshake was brief.

Mr. Moore turned his piercing, blue eyes on Violet. "Out to lunch?"

She swallowed. "Why, yes. Franki…ah, that is, Franklin and I haven't seen each other in years. He came to town for his niece's funeral."

A wince and a softening of Mr. Moore's eyes reflected in his words. "That must be Miss Shelton. So sorry to hear of her passing. A tragic loss, her being so young."

His kindness warmed Violet's heart. How did he, a busy businessman, know of a young woman who'd passed? It was evident to Violet that he had a caring heart.

Frankie nodded, his face serious, which made him look older. "Thank you. We will miss her greatly."

A few moments of awkwardness stilted the conversation, then Mr. Moore asked, "Holly must be tending the shop?"

Violet swallowed down the jumble in her gut, a guilty feeling, perhaps, for scheming against Mr. Moore's company. "Yes. It's so nice to be able to step out for a bit, knowing I've left the shop in good hands."

His eyes searched Violet's, and she could tell Mr. Moore—how she wanted to call him Devon—held something back.

"I know she's happy to be there," he said.

Another awkward silence.

Finally, Mr. Moore said, "I'll let you be on your way." He glanced at Frankie. "Nice to meet you."

Frankie nodded and smiled. "And you."

Mr. Moore moved quickly past them, and they were left standing in the hotel's foyer, the smell of lilies drifting to Violet from the bouquet on the front desk that she had made and that Webster had delivered yesterday.

Frankie spoke up and tugged on her arm. "Should we?"

Violet nodded and walked beside him. He held the door for her, and she exited first. He followed.

"So, that's *the* Mr. Moore?" Frankie asked, when they were outside.

"Yes."

"I have to say, he seems like a nice chap." Frankie eyeballed her. "Seems about as far removed from being a murderer as a kitten would be."

Violet brought her hand to her chest, shocked. "My goodness, I never meant to imply that Mr. Moore was personally involved with Roger's death. I can't imagine he knows what has gone on. I feel I know the kind of man he is. I've gotten to speak with him on several occasions."

Frankie winked at her. "Oh? He a regular customer?"

"No, well…" Again, Violet couldn't get her words out. *Grrr*, she growled internally. "It's just that with his niece working at the shop and all."

Frankie laughed. "No need to explain yourself. Come on. I should get you back to see if said shop is still standing."

Violet had a sinking feeling she would have to apologize for being late twice in one day, unheard of for her. Poor Holly. Violet hoped nothing had gone amiss in her absence. If so, she'd blame only herself.

Violet laughed in return. "Yes, let's."

Her heeled boots kept time with Frankie's lanky lope, as they made their way to Fragrant Sentiments. All the while, Violet scoured through the men she knew, wondering again whom she could label an admirer.

I know a place where the sun is like gold,
and the cherry blossoms burst with snow,
and down underneath is the loveliest nook,
where the four-leaf clovers grow.

Ella Higginson

CHAPTER SIX

Violet hiked up the wicker basket on her arm then reached down to lift her deep-lavender-colored skirt as she made her way through the tall grass. Decaying leaves mixed with the faint, fresh scent of growing things cheered Violet's heart. Not that she entertained melancholy, but her heart was lighter being amongst nature.

She paused where the prairie ended and the wooded property of their home began, a few miles west out of town. *Just mine now,* Violet realized. Nothing belonged to her *and* Roger anymore. The thought saddened her.

She had not been back to the wooded area where

Roger had died, but she longed to see the violets she knew grew there. And Frankie had wanted her to revisit the spot, to see if a memory would trigger some important, forgotten piece of information. Violet had her doubts about that.

Placing a hand on her straw hat to keep it secure in the breeze, Violet let her gaze roam around her. She sucked in a breath, and a sense of awe flooded through her like a shiver, making the hair on her arms stand up.

A carpet of purple violas covered the ground underneath the trees and spilled out into the field which she and Roger had turned into a small prairie, featuring different wildflowers, blooming May through September. The idea that something so lovely flourished where something so tragic had happened didn't make sense to Violet.

Peace washed over her, in spite of that fact. The thought that Roger now lived in the garden of his dreams led her to smile. *Roger.* He'd been the kindest and gentlest of men, and he had not deserved to die in such a cruel and senseless way. Violet could admit that a point of contention between her and God still existed. Try as she might, Violet could not relinquish what had happened over to The Almighty, the master of fates and the ultimate judge.

Yes, she still believed in God and all that Jesus came to do, she still prayed, still hoped, but the vow she held in her heart would not be uprooted. Violet had tried, but instead, it grew. Maybe now that she had Frankie helping her, they would uncover answers, and she could finally put the whole thing to rest.

Please, God, she prayed, knowing that she needed release from the burden. After all, wasn't there something in the Bible about not making foolish vows? At least one verse in Ecclesiastes, Violet recalled, but she shook the remembrance of it away.

Stooping down, Violet put the basket down on a mossy rock and slipped a paring knife out of it. She began to cut bunches of violets, bundling them in tussie mussies, tying them with strings she had pre-cut and put in the basket before she had left the flower shop. She had also pre-dampened some moss, to use as a bed in the bottom of the basket to keep the violets fresh. The violet bundles wouldn't keep long but would give herself and her customers a few days of joy.

After she bundled the tiny bouquets, she tucked them into the basket, upright and sandwiched between bunches of moss. Violets carried the calling card of a sweet, light fragrance of spring. Lowering her head down to smell deeper, Violet heard a disturbance. A flutter of wings and the twitter of birds above made her look up. A twig snapped, and Violet turned to look in that direction.

Webster approached, carrying a basket of his own, a wide-eyed look on his face. "Mrs. Brooks, Violet, I didn't think you'd be out here."

It surprised Violet to see her hired hand, but his presence also gave her a bit of comfort. Webster, Web for short, was familiar, easy to get along with, and not one for a lot of words, a lot like Violet that way. Her gaze rolled over her younger friend and employee. Even in his baggy bib overalls, Violet could decipher his lean, muscular body. He had a large forehead, which he tried to hide with his thick shock of sand-colored hair. Violet met his narrow eyes, which never settled on one thing for too long.

"It seems we are like-minded this morning." Violet stood up and groaned at the pinch she felt in her back. "Oof, spent too long cramped in that position. I'm getting old."

He held up his basket, a ring of disappointment in his voice. "I wanted to surprise you with a basket of violets, and…" he swallowed and looked her in the eye, "I don't see you as old."

Violet let the comment on her age pass and asked the question on her mind. "But how did you know they were here? The violets?"

She cocked her head sideways and lowered one brow. She had never discussed this spot with Web. Violet had thought of it as her own secret spot in the woods. She could imagine a troop of fairies playing among the blooms and mossy rocks.

Web itched behind an ear and swallowed. "Last spring…well, that is to say…ah, shucks, Mr. Brooks told me about them being here, and that aside from being your name, they were your favorite flower. That is, before he…you know." Web made a feeble gesture in the air, his wrist pivoting in a circle. He sighed. "I just wanted to do something nice for you, as you're so kind to me."

Violet didn't consider herself an overly kind person, but she did see people's needs and she liked to help. A neighbor's son, Webster had been around Violet and Roger for years and had often come into their gardens for one reason or another, a lost ball, to pass on something his mother had baked, to search for insects for a school project, and on the list went. It had been only natural that at some point—and Violet couldn't pinpoint when—Web had started working with them. The arrangement fit well for Violet and Roger, and for Web too. He had not wanted to go away to college, because he didn't want to leave his mother, Mrs. Polinski, alone. Violet knew that Web's father had died some years back and they had struggled financially for years.

"That's very thoughtful, Web. I appreciate that so much, but I think I have enough here." Violet tilted her basket to expose the many bunches of violets that she had tucked within it. She held out the basket. "Why don't you carry this for me. Walking through this tall grass is difficult with a basket full of flowers in one hand and my skirts bundled in another."

Violet extended her arm and with it her basket to Web. He took it.

He brightened and a smile broke out on his face, transforming him back into the boy Violet had known in years past for a few seconds. "Sure."

Then his huge strides through the grass reminded Violet that Webster was almost twenty years old and a man. Violet followed him, and they arrived back at the mown path through the prairie. Violet asked for her basket back.

"I can carry it to your buggy for you," he protested.

Violet twiddled her fingers and reached for the violet-laden basket. "I'm perfectly capable."

Web relinquished the basket. "All right. I'll finish cutting those lupines you wanted for the shop and stop them by in about an hour."

Violet wondered about the more direct gaze of his hazel eyes on her and the way his thin lips fell a little slack. It gave her the oddest feeling.

"Are you all right?" Violet asked him.

"Of course."

Web dropped his gaze, sounding irritated.

"See you later," he said as he turned and marched away.

For the life of her, Violet couldn't understand Web's strange behavior. Maybe something was wrong at home with his mother. Violet decided to make it a point to visit Mrs. Polinski as soon as she was able. That might shed light on the situation, Webster being talkative one minute and silent and moody the next. Violet had taken Web to be a pleasant and light-hearted young man, but not recently. *Well, not for a while.*

Violet shook her head and sighed, stowing her

basket in her buggy. She undid Milly's lead from the hitching post and kept the gray horse at a steady trot back to town. She realized along the way that she'd forgotten to look for anything to collaborate her suspicions about the Moore and Peterson Lumber Company. It would have to wait for another day. Maybe Frankie could go with her.

When Violet arrived back at the shop, Holly said goodbye and left for the day. Violet settled into her routine of finishing orders for the next day and doing afternoon paperwork. Web had come and gone without interrupting her, for which she was grateful. The clock neared 6:00, her evening closing time, and Violet looked forward to heading home, maybe making some eggs for supper and settling on her back porch swing afterwards with a Thomas Hardy novel.

But the best laid plans. Violet heard the doorbell ring and sighed. She'd have to serve one more customer before she could leave. She hurried to the door, to greet whoever entered and lock the door behind them, so she'd get no further walk-ins. A cringe ricocheted through her when she saw it was Mr. Clemons, also known as "Stanley Bear."

"Mr. Clemons, how can I help you?" Violet asked him, hoping he would not be purchasing two bouquets like he had last time.

Not that she didn't desire the extra sale, but she couldn't stand the thought of those women being duped by such an adulterous, mousy little man. With as much subtlety as she could muster, Violet maneuvered around him and twisted the lock on the door.

His face flushed red, and his small mouth puckered. "I demand my money back!"

One of his index fingers shot in the air. He waggled it in Violet's direction.

Violet batted her lashes and stood baffled in front of him. "I don't understand."

"Your incompetent aide mixed up my order. My bouquets went to the wrong addresses." His steel-colored, beady eyes hardened. "You can't imagine the grief I've endured because of it."

Violet lifted one eyebrow, giving him the kind of look her mother had bestowed on her when she had been guilty of something. "I'm sure I can't imagine. I apologize for any inconvenience. If you had sealed the envelopes, this would not have happened."

Violet went on to explain how the messages had fallen out and she had directed Holly which to pair with which bouquet.

He stuck his pointed nose in the air and pinned Violet with a superior eye. "Hmm, well. See that it does not happen next time I place an order."

They stared at each other for a few seconds, before Violet told him, in her most serious voice, "I'm not sure there will be a next time."

Mr. Clemons gasped.

This time Violet did not repent her tendency to speak before thinking. Granted, it wasn't good business to refuse custom, but she, in good conscience, could not accept continued business and money from a wormy little man cheating on his wife.

Mr. Clemons blinked at her. "Are you telling me that you are refusing my future business?"

He stuck out his neck, and it gave Violet the distinct impression of a turtle, stretching his neck out of his shell.

"Yes, I'm afraid I am," Violet told him, firm in her decision but hoping there wouldn't be negative repercussions.

Sticking out his chin, he said, "Humph, well I never! You'll be sorry. I'll tell everyone that I know what a poorly run business this is."

He turned without waiting for any response from Violet and marched a few feet back to the door, which he tried to open, only ending up rattling it.

Violet swept by him. "It's locked; allow me."

She unlocked the door and pushed it open. Mr. Clemons exited the shop, skewering Violet with a nasty stare on the way by.

"Good riddance," Violet couldn't help uttering after she had closed the door, but a smidgen of fear leaked into her heart as she wondered what Mr. Clemons might say about her and Fragrant Sentiments.

She could have blackmailed the man, demanding he

rein in his options, or Violet would reveal all to his wife. But perhaps the wife knew already. And Violet would never resort to blackmail to protect her reputation. She hoped and prayed she had done the right thing.

Lowering her gaze to the floor for a few moments while she offered up a quick prayer, Violet saw something white on the floor by the door. She walked to where it lay, wedged under a corner of the mat. She bent to pick it up and studied the envelope. Her name was penned in black ink, in a scrolling cursive, the same as the note she'd received a few days ago.

Violet inspected the area of the floor around where the note had been. Nothing appeared to have been disturbed. More than likely, the note had been pushed through the mailbox. Bending down by the door, her eyes level with the mail flap, Violet levered open the swinging, metal door on the slot a few times. It didn't make a sound, and it usually squeaked. Then she spied a glistening of oil on the hinge of the flap.

Someone oiled it, and I didn't do it. It had to have been someone who had come to the shop that day. Or Holly? *No,* Violet reasoned. Holly didn't know where she kept the oil can, and she couldn't see Holly bringing her own into the shop to use. Holly, most certainly, was not the kind of young woman to have a spare oil can stashed somewhere about her person.

Violet tallied up the customers who had been in the shop that day; none were likely candidates. The only other person Violet could count on her list of possible suspects was Web, but surely, if he were her secret admirer, he'd have found a better spot to deliver love notes than through the mail flap.

Then a thought hit her; Violet supposed the flap could have been oiled days ago, and she had just noticed it now. Tucking the thought away and curious about what the missive contained, Violet wanted to open it, but playing a game she wasn't sure she wished to be a part of tired her. She let out a quiet groan and opened it anyway. The blood gushed in her ears as she read the few lines out loud.

"Dear Violet, if only I could express my true feelings to you, outright, But first, I must win your admiration, at a distance, not imposing my love upon you but opening the door gently. In this I hope to suggest the possibility of more than a cursory knowledge of each other. I entertain the thought of something more and the hope that perhaps, someday, you'll be mine. Until next time, your secret admirer."

The words both shocked and elated Violet. She ran her finger carefully over the four-leaf clover, glued by the signature on the note. In the language of flowers, clover symbolized a connection, a longing to belong, and an ability to be true to oneself. It made Violet happy to think that the writer of the note seemed to signify that he saw this quality in her. She hoped she would always hold true to her convictions and commitments. That's why she'd told Mr. Clemons no and why she couldn't relinquish her vow to Roger. Not yet.

Turning the paper over, Violet examined it as she had the last note to look for any clues as to the author, but she found nothing.

Who can it be? The question rang in her head, calling for answers, but again she had none. Someone among her friends or acquaintances held her in the highest possible regard to etch and deliver such words of love to her. The whole idea left Violet flummoxed. She had not been seeking love, but apparently love had found her.

She folded the paper up and tucked it in her pocket, a warm current spreading throughout her body at the idea that someone loved her and expressed that care in such a deeply romantic gesture. She imagined herself being a character in a Shakespearean play. With light steps, Violet shut the shop up and hurried to the livery to get Milly for their ride home. She hummed a tune the whole time, feeling lighter in spirit than she had in months.

*Love is like wildflowers; it's often found
in the most unlikely places.*

Ralph Waldo Emerson

CHAPTER SEVEN

Frankie shook his head and lifted one side of his lips up in a dissatisfied smirk. "This is all I could wrangle up, I'm afraid. Not much to go on, to be sure."

He laid a paper down on Violet's desk. Frankie had stopped by Fragrant Sentiments a few minutes ago to accompany her to lunch.

"I talked with the clerk in the office. He did confirm that a," Frankie turned the paper with a finger and read toward the top, "Mr. Cole had been out by your property and sent a team to do some preliminary surveying. Know him?"

Violet shook her head. "I didn't get a name."

Frankie scratched at his jawline. "Shucks. That's right." He turned the paper back in Violet's direction.

"We still got the general store owner. He told me that he found a receipt for a steel trap, bought last May. The only problem is he doesn't know who bought it. The man must've paid with cash not credit, so the man's name or address wasn't given. I asked for a physical description, but the store owner said his niece had been helping him out in the store that day and that he'd have to write and ask her if she remembered anything about the purchase." Shrugging his sturdy shoulders, Frankie confessed, "It's a long shot but something at least."

Violet nodded but didn't speak. She didn't want to reveal the disappointment she felt as a result of how little information Frankie had turned up. What were they supposed to do now?

"Will you still be able to do an article on the lumber company?" Violet asked him.

Frankie shook his head and rubbed his clean-shaven chin. "Nah, doesn't look promising. I interviewed a few employees, but they didn't have anything bad to say about the company. When I mentioned Mr. Moore, however, that raised a few eyebrows."

Violet swallowed, her throat feeling suddenly dry. "How do you mean?"

"Well, no one gave specifics, but one man indicated Mr. Moore had stolen another man's identity."

Violet couldn't help herself and gasped before masking her shock with a cough. "That doesn't make sense. What could he have meant?"

She didn't get to hear Frankie's answer. The

doorbell jangled, and a customer walked into Fragrant Sentiments—a regular, whom Violet knew required prompt assistance and would only wish to be helped by Violet and not Holly.

Sighing, Violet told Frankie, "It'll have to keep for another day. I must go help my customer."

She rose from her desk chair and walked over to Frankie.

"Should we reschedule our lunch date?" he asked.

"That might be best. Tomorrow?"

Violet again tried to imagine Frankie writing the heartfelt words in the love notes she had received. It didn't seem possible, but then people did surprise once in a while.

His eyes found hers. "Meet you here or at the hotel?"

Violet had enjoyed renewing her friendship with Frankie and wanted to continue to do so. "I wish you could stay longer."

She touched his arm.

"Yooo hoo, Mrs. Brooks," the warbly voice of Miss Celia Ryan, one of the local, well-to-do spinsters, called from the sales floor.

Violet waved at her. "Be with you in a moment, Miss Ryan." She turned to Frankie. "I'm sorry. I must go. I'll see you tomorrow at the hotel at noon."

Spinning around, Violet moved to go, but Frankie caught her hand.

His eyes softened and focused on Violet's. "I'll meet you here, and we can walk together, yes?"

Violet ignored the look of supplication in Frankie's eyes.

"Fine," she agreed.

It was as if he asked for more than a lunch date, but she wasn't certain. She flashed a smile and squeezed his fingers before pulling away from his grasp.

"Tomorrow," she heard him say as she slipped from her office area and approached her customer to discuss with her which flowers would be best to grace Miss Ryan's dining room table.

While talking, Violet's eyes followed Frankie as he left the shop. She had spoken the absolute truth. She would be sad to see him go, but did that sadness come from a sort of romantic notion about Frankie? It would take her more time before Violet could say with any honesty what feelings she harbored for him, but they didn't have much time. All too soon Frankie would head back to Chicago, and where would that leave her?

After helping Miss Ryan select some deep maroon sweet Williams, pink peonies, and white delphinium, Violet asked Holly to wrap them up, glad to pass on the gossipy woman.

Poor Holly. She'd get an earful of everything she might want to know and much more, but the price of running a shop amounted to tolerating their customers' idiosyncrasies, if gossip could be labeled as such.

Violet set to work, creating some floral arrangements that could be bought and taken with her walk-in customers. She liked to have a few such things on hand for those who did not have time to call ahead and order or to wait while she made an arrangement. Many people did not plan ahead but waited, as if it were an afterthought, to purchase flowers for an occasion.

Her mind wound down from the flurry it had been in, talking to Frankie and helping Miss Ryan, and Violet settled into her well-loved, comfortable groove of designing. It brought her much peace and joy to arrange flowers, God's beautiful creations, in a pleasing design— sometimes as the flowers might grow together in nature and other times in more stylized groupings. Humming as she worked, Violet soon finished one arrangement of pink and yellow flowers and moved on to another.

Holly approached and bent over, leaning one elbow on the worktable. "I've finished with the morning chore list and Miss Ryan. Anything else you'd like me to work on?"

Holly's dark eyes and smile were as calm and sweet as ever.

Really, Violet had expected Holly to fizzle out and not be up for the labor behind the romantic appeal of Fragrant Sentiments, but to her credit, Holly had done well. More than well. She seemed to flourish, here among the plants and flowers, to say nothing of her skill as a saleswoman. Cranky Mrs. Etna, who rarely bought anything, came in yesterday, and by the time she left, Holly had sold her two arrangements, a basket of soaps, and a box of hankies, embroidered with different flowers.

Violet smiled, pleased with her new employee, who was also fast becoming a friend. "Thank you so much, Holly."

She thought of what jobs she could have Holly do, then she remembered the shipment she'd received yesterday and hadn't had time to open yet.

Violet pointed to the back of the shop. "Out behind the shop, there are several large crates of ceramic and clay pots for plants. I'd like you to open them and price them for me. There's an invoice on my desk with the appropriate pricing. There's also a sketched image of the different style pots so you know how to match up the pots with the correct price. Tags are on my desk too."

Standing up straight, Holly smiled sweetly. "Certainly, I'll gladly do that. It looks like such a lovely day. I'll be happy to be outside for a while."

Is Holly ever in a poor mood? Violet had a hard time imagining it.

"Thank you," Violet simply stated.

Holly gave a nod and marched off with her orders. Violet finished a few more small arrangements and was on her last when the doorbell rang, and someone entered the shop. She looked to see who it was. Her eyes lit on *Mr. Devon Moore.*

Watching Mr. Moore entering the shop caused a flutter in Violet's chest; the man made her nervous. He walked forward with a smile to the table Violet worked at, arranging pink peonies and pink roses in a vase with greens clipped from her forsythia bush and ferns she foraged for in the woods.

Violet smiled back, trying not to appear too eager to see him. "Good morning, Mr. Moore. Here to accompany Holly home, again?"

Though thinking it odd that he rarely left his niece unattended, Violet again considered his loving attachment to Holly. What other uncle would be so attentive? But Violet remembered that Holly's parents had passed. Holding on to what little family you had was important to most people.

He smiled, a handsome, even curve underneath his trim mustache. "Yes." He answered Violet's question, then his eyes dimmed from their usual sparkle. Looking around the sales floor, he asked, "Where is my niece?"

Violet pointed again. "Out, behind the shop. She's sorting and pricing a shipment of pots I received." With a direct gaze, Violet asked, "Would you like me to fetch her?"

Mr. Moore shook his head. "Oh, no. Don't interrupt her work. I can wait."

Violet nodded but wondered whether she should converse with him or if he'd rather browse around the sales floor.

Clearing his throat, Mr. Moore said, "This will give us an opportunity to get to know each other better."

He smiled again, one cheek rising higher, scrunching the skin around his eye, making it appear significantly smaller than the other one. His words rang with sincerity and not simply politeness.

"I'd like that," Violet said, hoping her words didn't sound too eager.

With his eyes attentive to her, he asked, "Do you love it?"

The direct question took Violet by surprise. "You mean the shop?"

"Of course," he answered, his eyes still trained on hers.

She met his intent eyes then focused on adding another peony to the vase in front of her. "I do. I certainly adore working with flowers."

He stepped a little closer to her. "But?"

That one word threw her. He seemed able to read her.

She decided to be honest. "If I only had to manage the flowers and make arrangements, I'd be thrilled. It's selling them that's the challenge."

To be brutally honest, Violet preferred flowers to people most days, but she thought sharing that might sound too stand-offish.

Mr. Moore placed both of his elbows on the high worktable and wove his fingers across his middle. "You appear to be doing well for yourself, but I'm sure you miss your husband. Holly told me he died about a year ago."

His tone didn't pry. He opened an opportunity for Violet to talk about Roger and her life, but Violet wasn't prepared to discuss Roger with Mr. Moore. Not yet anyway. She might say something she regretted, and she wanted to have some facts to back up her suspicions.

"I am managing. I'm thankful for the help I have in my staff, but you're correct; I do miss my husband, Roger."

His head tipped down. "The grief over the loss of a spouse must be grave." Mr. Moore focused on Violet and continued, "I can only imagine such a thing."

Every time Violet spoke with Holly's uncle, their conversations skirted around some center topic that wasn't named but presented itself all the same. Violet found it both maddening and exciting, rather like a mystery waiting to be uncovered.

That's what Mr. Devon Moore is—a mystery.

Violet caught a warm glint in his blue eyes, like the sky blue of a summer's day. "It has been, but staying busy here in the shop sure has helped."

They shared a smile, then he cleared his throat. "While I wait, might you give me a tour of your shop? I am curious about the inner workings."

He glanced at the flower arrangement she worked on. Violet still held her knife in her hand.

He waited then said, "That is, unless you are too busy."

Violet blinked, not sure what to tell him. "There's not much to it, I'm afraid. We grow some flowers and plants, ship others in, and do our best to sell them." Moving from behind the worktable, Violet laid her knife on the counter and motioned with her arm. "I'll gladly give you a brief tour, and after, we'll check on Holly." Violet looked down at her watch pinned to her shirtwaist. Holly had been outside for an hour. "She should be almost finished by now."

"Wonderful, lead the way."

Mr. Moore stepped back, and Violet brushed by him. She sniffed the manly smell of clove, amber, and bergamot on him, a welcome blend.

"This way."

Violet led him around her small domain, and he commented on each flower and gift-line she mentioned. It seemed that the same attentiveness she saw in him applied to more than the object of his niece. She liked a man who listened. It had been one of the character qualities she had loved the most about Roger. When she had something to tell him or simply needed a listening ear, he had been there, doing just that— listening.

They reached the back wall, where Violet kept backstock of supplies, buckets, and pots.

A twinkle sparkled at the outer corner of his eye, perhaps reflecting off the electric lightbulb, hanging from the ceiling. "Now, tell me. What makes you happy, here amidst your flower shop?"

Again, it surprised her that he showed interest in her happiness. It revealed an earmark of selflessness. As a result, her fondness for him instantly grew.

She tilted her head and gave Mr. Moore a sideways glance. "Using a beautiful product of God's handiwork to create arrangements. That makes me happy." Feeling brave, she asked, "And what makes Mr. Devon Moore happy?"

He didn't hesitate. "Holly. She's blessed my life beyond measure this year. She's basically all the family I have left. My parents and brother died years ago...and also someone special I cared for." He puckered up his lips and paused for several seconds. "I have some cousins on my father's side but have never met any of them."

He shrugged and gave Violet that sad smile she'd seen before.

"Family is a gift. I too have lost my parents. I have siblings who live in Minnesota, Wisconsin, and Iowa, but rarely see them. One of my sisters still lives in the area. We visit from time to time." Violet signaled with a graceful arch of her hand. "The back door is there."

She directed ahead and began leading the way.

"Right." With grace Mr. Moore stepped to the back door and opened it. "Allow me."

He held it open for her, and Violet walked through the open doorway into the fenced-in area behind the shop.

Mr. Moore followed her, and he visited with Holly while she finished her last few pots. Violet studied them together, not able to see what Frankie had insinuated—that Mr. Moore was a liar and a cheat. The old thread of gossip about him had to be false. Within a matter of minutes, they all walked back into the shop, and Holly bid Violet a good day after collecting her hat and bag. Mr. Moore held open the front door, and Holly exited with a wave. Expecting him to follow, Violet stood waiting.

He paused by her side. "Ah, I would welcome the opportunity to visit with you more, Mrs. Brooks. Would you join me soon for lunch or perhaps an afternoon tea, if it doesn't interrupt your workday too much?"

Violet swallowed. *Two men wanting to have lunch with me?*

She almost laughed out loud but instead succumbed to the lightheadedness that came over her. In a half swoon, she put the back of her hand to her forehead. Heaven help her; she was acting like a love-sick school girl. She pulled in a breath.

Concern stitched Mr. Moore's eyes and brow into a pucker. "Are you quite all right, Mrs. Brooks?"

He reached out a hand to her, but Violet flicked her hand at him.

"Oh, it's nothing. Really. I get a little lightheaded when I skip lunch."

She didn't look him in the eye.

He stood still, smiling. "All the more reason to accept my invitation. Please."

This time she looked into those handsome eyes of his, and the tug on her heart could not be denied.

"Yes," she blurted out, her cheeks heating at the embarrassment of her girlishness.

Grinning, he exposed a fine set of teeth. "Wonderful, I'll stop by to escort you to Grapevine Lodge at a quarter to noon, if that time is convenient for you."

Violet nodded. *I'll be going to the Lodge?*

She had always wanted to see inside the sprawling mansion. "Thank you. I'll look forward to it."

"I will as well," he said.

With a smile and a tap of his straw hat, Mr. Moore followed his niece and left the shop. Again, Violet stood by the door and watched them, imagining herself with them, making up a trio.

Violet gasped as a thought hit her. *I'm supposed to be having lunch with Frankie tomorrow!*

She groaned. How had she gotten herself into this pickle of a predicament?

Life is a flower,
of which love is the honey.

Victor Hugo

CHAPTER EIGHT

Violet ended up canceling lunch with Frankie to meet Mr. Moore. She hadn't lied to Frankie but had said that something had come up. However, she still felt bad.

Now on Devon's arm—Mr. Moore had insisted she call him by his first name—Violet could almost imagine herself a lady of significant social standing, being led through such a fine home. Violet kept her house and decor as stylish as she could, but her efforts paled in comparison to the elaborate woodworking and trim of the home, to say nothing of the sparkling crystal chandeliers, beautifully printed wallpaper, and elegant furnishings.

The surroundings did nothing to alleviate her nerves about having a meal with Devon but made Violet feel like an upstart, trying to grasp a rung too far above her rank in society.

Devon pulled out a dining chair, upholstered in green fabric with a textural fern design. "Allow me."

Violet sat on the chair, and he helped her push it in.

"Thank you," she told him.

Lightweight, white curtains fluttered in the breeze in the airy room, decorated in shades of green and white. Potted ferns accented the two corners of the room by the bank of east-facing windows. A honey-stained, modest-sized, oak table, laid with white linens and dishes, edged in gold, stretched on either side of Violet, and a crystal chandelier hung overhead. It was a beautiful room.

Devon walked around the table. "I thought we might be more comfortable in the morning room for our luncheon."

He pulled out a chair opposite Violet, his gaze fixed on her, even as he sat down.

"This isn't the dining room?" Violet asked.

If such was the case, she couldn't imagine what a formal dining room might look like in this mansion of a home.

One side of Devon's mouth rose in a half smile. "No. It's far too large for an intimate meal."

"Oh," Violet said in a soft voice, embarrassed at her ignorance.

Having grown up in a family where her needs had been met but wants were rarely indulged, an uncomfortable and imaginary weight pressed on Violet's chest. It had always bothered her—growing up poor.

Roger had looked past her humble upbringing, and Violet had partaken of the things of life she had only dreamed about before she met him, like more than one or two dresses to wear, a pair of shoes that didn't pinch or have holes, her own room, and food on her plate at every meal.

Concern shadowed his graying brows, and Devon went to the sideboard, which stood against one wall. "Let me pour you a glass of water. Perhaps the midday sun on our walk here overheated you. You look flushed."

He poured water from a glass pitcher into a cut-glass tumbler. Walking up to Violet, he handed it to her.

"Thank you."

Violet took it, drank a sip of water, and set the glass down on the table. A little voice in her head kept telling her, *You don't belong here.* However, she tuned it out as best as she could and made an effort to focus on Devon and not herself. She started a different thread of conversation.

"How are all the preparations coming for Holly's wedding?" Violet asked. "I can't believe it's less than two weeks away. I really don't know how I'll manage without her in the shop, when she's off."

Giving a slight nod, Mr. Moore pulled his lips back in a sideways smile. "Oh, good. We will borrow some chairs from the First Presbyterian Church in town.

Holly wanted to get married here at Grapevine Lodge in the garden, so that's what I arranged."

Violet's anxiety eased, talking about weddings and flowers, two things she knew much about, being in the budding floral industry. "That'll be lovely. Might I see the garden? It will help me to have the setting in mind when I design the bouquets."

Those bright blue eyes of his widened, like he sought contrition for his oversight. "Certainly. I don't know why I didn't think to offer a tour before. I apologize."

"That's not necessary. Really, I should have asked. Holly mentioned it would be outside but didn't tell me where. And I recall the day we were discussing it at the shop; we became sidetracked by a customer."

Violet didn't elaborate, as a servant brought in a tray of plated food.

Devon smiled at the middle-aged woman with frizzy, red hair held back in a bun and said, "Wonderful. Thank you, Mrs. Porter."

Her grumpy expression brightened. "You're welcome, sir." She flashed a slight smile, making her appear younger, and set the tray down, glancing at Violet. "Ma'am."

Violet nodded in return.

Devon gestured Violet's way. "Oh, Mrs. Porter, let me introduce you to Mrs. Violet Brooks, owner of the flower shop downtown. Violet, this is my proficient housekeeper, Mrs. Porter."

Violet received the same kind of lopsided smile from

her, accompanied by a wary glint in Mrs. Porter's hazel eyes.

"Happy to make your acquaintance, Mrs. Brooks."

"Likewise," Violet muttered, holding the impression Mrs. Porter had cast judgment upon her and found her wanting.

"Thank you again, Mrs. Porter. You may leave the tray," said Devon, with a pleasantness in his tone.

Mrs. Porter didn't protest and left the room, but not before sending Violet another strange look. Perhaps the woman thought her a fortune hunter, out to catch her employer in a snare.

Devon set one plate of sandwiches, canned fruit, and a wedge of some kind of cake before Violet. "Here we are."

Nothing too extravagant. She was glad.

"Thank you," Violet told him, waiting until he had his plate before him to take a bite of her food.

It surprised her when Devon asked if he could say grace. She nodded, a bit shy, and listened while he offered up a heartfelt prayer of gratitude. And Violet liked him even more.

"Amen," she echoed him, and they began eating.

Talking with Devon came easier than Violet had expected. Soon, she had told him about Roger, how they had met, the plans they had had for years of opening a flower shop, and how much she hoped she could keep the shop in operation.

Violet flipped the conversation and gently probed

into his life. "May I ask why you and Holly seem unusually close for an uncle and niece? It's as if you are father and daughter."

Devon wiped his mouth with the napkin on his lap. He looked down at the table and tinkered with his fork. "That's definitely how I feel toward Holly—like she's my daughter, but…she isn't, you see. She is my brother's daughter. William…"

Devon paused again, clearly uncomfortable dredging up old memories.

"He died in an accident when Holly was only ten years old." Devon looked her in the eye for a few seconds then dropped his gaze to the table again. "I'm ashamed to say that out of grief I stayed away from home for far too long. Holly lived with her mother's sister, Nel, and her husband during that time."

"She told me." Violet said the words with understanding and a warmth she hoped he could sense.

"What else did she tell you?" he asked, in a sudden burst, with a tinge of something akin to fear.

Violet watched his Adam's apple bob and his blue eyes glisten but not with joy. No, unshed tears. *What trunk of painful memories have I disturbed?*

"Not much at all. Why?" Violet asked, keeping her tone steady.

A memory of Frankie mentioning something about a stolen identity flickered in her mind. What that could mean if it were true left Violet wondering.

How do I bring that up? Violet thought about the

problem. Maybe a question like that would go too far. Presume too much.

Clearing his throat loudly, Devon sat up straight, seemingly over his lapse into emotion. "I think I'll leave that answer for another day. Let me give you a quick tour of the garden and escort you back to your shop."

He stood and wasted no time in rounding the table and helping Violet up.

In minutes Devon showed her the clipped lawn behind the lodge, hedged in with borders of flowering bushes of all sorts and a few sections where some perennials like foxglove, bleeding heart, trillium, violets, and peonies grew. Violet recognized the greenery of other perennials that would bloom later in the summer, echinacea, heuchera, and rudbeckia.

"It's a lovely spot," she told him.

The same sadness in his voice she had heard before leaked out with his words, as he told Violet, "I think Holly's mother and father would have been happy to see her say her wedding vows here."

As if by reflex, Violet reached out her hand to him, and he took it. "I'm sorry they won't be able to witness her day."

The pressure of his manly fingers around hers was a welcome sensation, and the companionship she felt with him brought her a new element of joy she had missed for some time. She thought of Roger but thankfully didn't experience guilt for enjoying Devon's presence and touch.

They held hands until they reached the public sidewalk. Once there, Devon released her and offered her his arm, which she took. Their steps in tandem, neither of them spoke, and the peace of knowing Violet didn't have to fill the void endeared his company to her, yet again. Here was a man she could converse with and share the quiet with. Violet smiled and wrapped her hand more firmly around Devon's muscular forearm.

What's in a name?
That which we call a rose,
by any other name
would smell as sweet.

~

William Shakespeare

CHAPTER NINE

"What? Can't a sister stop by unannounced?"

Violet glared at her older sister Gwen. *Would it have been too much trouble for her to write, saying that she planned to come for a visit?*

"Some warning would have been nice. I have orders to fill and a wedding this week and one next. How long are you in town for, and where are Bernie and the girls?"

Gwen grinned like the Cheshire Cat of Lewis Carol's fantasy story. "Bernard took Lizzy and Penny to his folks for a few days. Melinda is vacationing with her best friend's family, and I decided to come visit you," she blew Violet an air kiss, "just because."

But Violet wasn't fooled by her flippancy. She could see Gwen held something back.

"And?" Violet asked.

She held a long-stemmed rose in mid-air, her knife clasped in her other hand. A vase of eleven red roses with plumosa fern waited in front of Violet on her worktable for its last addition. She searched the pale green—sage green, almost—of Gwen's eyes looking for the real reason she had come. Gwen never did anything on a whim; she liked to plan and hated surprises.

Gwen raised her voice. "And what? There's no AND!"

Thank goodness there was no one else in the shop but them. Holly had left for the day, and Webster was out doing a late delivery.

Placing the rose up high in the center of the arrangement of roses, Violet set her knife down and walked around the counter. "Tell me why you're really here."

Gwen raised her arms out to her sides, shrugging, before letting them fall back down.

"I'm bored," she blurted out. "Bernard's always gone, the girls need me less and less, and Melinda never needed me." Laughing, a ring of bitterness darkening the pitch, Gwen said, "Born an independent spirit that one."

"Well, maybe join a women's group or start a hobby," Violet suggested, but she was rather at a loss.

When has Gwen sought my advice for anything? Thinking hard, Violet couldn't pinpoint a single time.

Gwen shook her head. "No, no. You don't understand."

She dug in the groove of a scratch mark on the counter with a fingernail.

Violet recognized her own past restlessness in her sister's. Outwardly, they reflected each other, too, though Gwen sported fair hair and Violet dark. Their facial features, with pointy nose, petite face, even eyes, and a dainty chin spelled out their familial link.

"Make it clear. What is the trouble?" Violet asked.

She reached out and raised Gwen's chin, looking her square in the eye.

Shaking her head out of Violet's grasp, Gwen heaved out a discontented sigh and continued. "I have nothing that's mine. I don't know who I am anymore." With a heavy sigh, she went on, "It's easy for you. Even after Roger's passing you still have the flowers and your shop. What do I have?"

Violet realized her sister needed a good reminder of her blessings. "You have Bernie, the girls, and a lovely home."

"Yes, but don't you see? None of them *need* me. I have no role anymore."

With this statement, Gwen started to cry.

Violet patted Gwen on the shoulder. "There, there."

She took Gwen by the arm and led her to the consultation table and chairs by the display of green houseplants. She pulled out a chair and pushed Gwen into it. Violet sat as well.

Pulling a hankie out of her apron pocket, Violet

passed it to Gwen, who dabbed her nose with it. "I think you're wrong. Your family will always need you. Perhaps not as much or in different ways, but they will. Besides," Violet rubbed Gwen's arm, "you'll find an interest to pursue. I'm certain."

Gwen sniffed. "You think?"

In an effort to bolster her sister's spirits, Violet offered some suggestions. "Of course. You enjoy flowers too. What about expanding your gardens or trying to develop some hybrid blooms for a certain species? Perhaps you could teach gardening classes to a ladies' society group? Or what about tutoring? You were one of the smartest students in our school."

Lifting her gaze, Gwen blinked and cracked half a pathetic excuse for a smile. "I suppose."

The empty tone Violet heard in her sister's voice caused her to worry. *Is melancholy overtaking her?*

An idea popped into Violet's mind. "Say, it's almost closing time. I can close a little early. We'll go to my house and make pancakes for supper, like we used to do when we were children. What do you say?"

So many wonderful memories of her and Gwen as girls ran through Violet's head. *What happened to us? Why don't we do anything together anymore?*

Violet set her mind to changing that.

Gwen nodded. "I'd like that." She lifted her gaze up to Violet, her green eyes shining like polished chrysoprase. "I'm sorry for interrupting your day but I couldn't think of who else to turn to."

"That's what family is for," Violet assured her sister. She sent up a prayer of forgiveness for her earlier, ungracious thoughts about Gwen. "Want to help me put the flowers in the cool room?"

Gwen perked up. "Sure."

"Good. Follow me."

Violet picked up the vase of roses and was about to lead Gwen to the display of flowers in tin buckets when she remembered she needed to flip the open sign to closed and lock the front door of the shop.

"Could you go turn the sign and lock the door?" Violet asked. "I'll start on the buckets, and we'll be done in no time."

Gwen hesitated. "What happened to your busy day?"

"It can keep until tomorrow."

Gwen nodded and smiled. She walked to the door, and Violet went to the cool room with the vase of roses she held. After opening the door, she placed it on one of the wooden shelves inside that Roger had built. Stepping back out, she hurried to the flower display and grabbed some buckets.

Approaching Violet, Gwen held out an envelope. "I found this."

Violet recognized it instantly. *My secret admirer has struck again.*

She set the bucket she held on the floor and extended her hand to Gwen. "Ah, thanks. I'll tuck it into my pocket."

Gwen laid the note in Violet's outstretched palm but still held on to it at the corner with a couple of fingers. "Looks like expensive paper and such nice penmanship." Releasing the note, Gwen trailed the tip of her index finger over "*Violet*" scrolled out in back ink. "The sender must know you well."

With Gwen's relinquished hold, Violet took the opportunity to tuck the note into the waistband of her skirt, since she didn't have an apron on. "Nothing to concern you." Violet picked up the bucket and hurried to the cool room, tossing over her shoulder, "Grab a couple of buckets, please."

She really hoped Gwen wouldn't continue to quiz her about the note. That was all she needed—her big sister discovering that she had a secret admirer.

But no such luck existed. As Gwen and Violet finished with the flowers and Violet collected her things, Gwen plied her with one question after another until Violet confessed what she had been receiving.

Gwen winked and grinned wickedly. "Shameful. Seducing a widow."

Violet rubbed the envelope with a thumb, wondering what ardent words were etched inside this time. "It's nothing like that. Besides, it's been over a year since Roger passed."

Gwen waggled her fingers, her eyes big, and still that huge grin on her face. "Well, let's hear it."

Shocked, Violet's cheeks heated. "You want me to read it now?"

Such an eager look lit up Gwen's face; Violet reasoned it would give her sister some pleasure to learn more about Violet's penned love affair.

"What are sisters for?" Gwen asked.

Violet rolled her eyes at Gwen and pulled the note from her skirt. "Very well."

After unfolding it, Violet read it aloud in a rather bored voice, as if the professions of love meant nothing to her. The distinct fragrance of oil-of-rose perfumed her words.

"Dear Violet, I borrow from 'The Poet' today: a rose by any other name would surely not smell as sweet. You are a sweet fragrance to me, Violet, and I long to have the pleasure of your company, perfuming my days and hours, always. The lilt of your voice, clarity of your eyes, and enduring spirit speak to mine. With love, your admirer."

Violet lowered the paper, too aghast to share her thoughts with Gwen.

The man surely and truly is in love with me. Violet had thought it a passing fancy, a mild flirtation, but no. With this message, he signed it *with love.* She audibly groaned.

Gwen reached out and snatched the note from Violet's hands. "I have to say, this was worth leaving home for." She looked at the paper, likely reading it again to discover if Violet had held a juicy tidbit back. Apparently satisfied, Gwen handed it back to Violet. "Any idea who your secret lover is?"

Setting her mouth in a grim line, Violet said, "He is

not my *lover* and no, I do not know."

Gwen's expectant eyes remained on Violet. "But you can surely guess. Who are the candidates?"

"For what?" a distinctly male voice asked from behind them.

Violet clutched her hand over her hammering heart and swung around. Webster stood with his head at an angle, blinking at her.

"Web! You shouldn't creep up on a body like that."

He shook his head, sweat glistening on his brow. "I wasn't sneaking." The buttons of his shirt were undone toward the top, and smooth, tanned skin shone underneath, revealing barely a hair on his muscular-looking chest. "Just came to wish you a good evening before I head out. I'll see you tomorrow. I'll stop by the house early to water the gardens. Most of all, the roses need the moisture."

His eyes lingered on Violet's for a few seconds.

Roses. Violet narrowed her eyes and examined Webster, who was almost young enough to be her son. *Surely not. But stranger things have happened.*

Violet believed, as a businesswoman and his employer, to say nothing of their age difference, that if some attachment were to form between herself and Web, it would be highly inappropriate. And indeed, Gwen was right—scandalous.

Violet uttered a quiet, "Thank you, Webster."

She dropped her gaze and Webster turned in Gwen's direction.

Violet figured that she better introduce them. "Web…ah, Webster, this is my sister, Gwen. I'm sure you've met her before, but it was probably years ago." She turned to Gwen. "This is Mr. Webster Polinski, friend, employee, and all-round handyman."

Gwen whispered out of the side of her mouth, "I'll bet."

Violet cringed and squinted at her.

Rubbing at his chin, which sported a light stubble, Webster nodded. "Sure. I can see the resemblance. You do look familiar. Nice to make your acquaintance again, ma'am."

He touched his tweed cap and smiled at Gwen.

Gwen grinned back. "And yours, sir."

Although Violet wouldn't consider Webster to be conventionally handsome, he had an appeal about him, an easy kindness that made him comfortable to be around.

With his gaze now settled on Violet, Webster nodded again. "You ladies have a lovely evening."

A charge of something blistered the air as he passed by her, and the hair on Violet's arm stood up. Violet shook free of the odd sensation.

After he had turned and left, Gwen picked up her line of inquiry. "Clearly, we have candidate number one. Who's second in the running?"

Violet shook her head; she did not want to delve into this conversation.

With a little shimmy of her shoulders, Gwen tilted

her head. "Come on, 'fess up. I can tell from your high color that Webster is not the only possible choice."

Groaning silently, Violet thought she better get it over with. "There's Mr. Devon Moore."

Plunking her elbows down on the worktable, Gwen smiled. "Oh, I like the name Devon."

She hiked up her eyebrows. Violet gave her the barest of details about Devon.

"Will I get to meet him?" Gwen asked.

Violet shrugged. "Perhaps."

Standing up straight, Gwen rose off her elbows. Violet could see her sister had lost the forlorn expression she had worn when she walked into the shop.

"Any other contenders?"

Violet looked Gwen in the eye. "You're never going to believe this one."

She waited for maximum effect.

Gwen rolled her wrist and hand. "Who?"

"Do you remember Frankie?"

Gwen tapped her chin with an index finger. "Frankie?"

Violet waited for it to register. "Think back to school."

Gwen puckered her lips and screwed up her eyes. "Hmm, let's see. Frankie…" She turned wide eyes to Violet. "You don't mean Dodgy Dermot?"

Violet laughed. "I forgot he was called that. He's grown up into a respectable and responsible man, believe it or not, and become a journalist."

"I would never have guessed. He still live around here?" Gwen asked.

Moving to string her bag on her arm and turn the lights off, Violet herded Gwen toward the door. "No, he doesn't. Come to my place, and I'll tell you what brought Frankie back to town."

But Violet wasn't certain about revealing the project she and Frankie were working on to Gwen. Maybe. But not yet. Frankie had sent word he'd turned up nothing further talking with the men from Moore Lumber. Though he'd discovered Mr. Cole was a hard businessman through and through, he'd found nothing to suggest he'd stoop to such actions as laying a trap. He'd questioned the general store owner and her neighbors again too. All to no avail. What avenue they would try next, Violet wasn't sure. But she was no longer convinced someone from Moore Lumber was to blame.

Gwen collected the suitcase that she had left by the door, and she and Violet walked to the livery to hitch up Milly, their ride home. On the way, Violet reflected on how Gwen's unforeseen visit might be a blessing in disguise.

If I had a flower for every time I thought of you,
I could walk in my garden forever.

~

Alfred Lord Tennyson

CHAPTER TEN

Violet and Gwen had chatted away most of the night, reliving days past and dreaming about days ahead. They had turned in at a quarter to midnight. It made Violet so glad to have Gwen there with her. She didn't know why she had grumbled about her sister's visit.

The next morning, Violet opened the door, expecting the morning paper, but she found Devon, instead, holding berry-picking baskets.

He grinned and held up the baskets. "Good morning, I thought I'd stop by and see if you want to join me. The strawberries are ripe for the picking, down at Waitfields. What do you say?"

How could Violet say no to those blue eyes? Though she had a lot of work to do and...*Gwen.*

She sighed and leaned on the open door. "My sister, Gwen, is here for a visit. I'm afraid that I'll have to decline."

But oh, how she wanted to say yes! At least she could be glad that Devon looked as disappointed as she felt. Footsteps behind her made Violet turn her head.

"Someone say my name?" Gwen looked from Violet to Devon. "Aren't you going to introduce me?"

Her light green eyes shone the color of patinaed copper.

Great.

"Gwen, this is Mr. Devon Moore, and Devon, this is my sister, Gwen."

Violet made the introduction as brief as possible. She made to clamp her hands on Gwen's shoulders and turn her around, but Devon stuck out his free hand.

"I can see the family resemblance. So nice to meet you, Gwen."

Gwen shook his hand and said, "Likewise." She smiled mischievously and pegged her eyes on Violet. "Don't let me stop you from enjoying a little free time. I'll be here when you get back, and work can wait. Besides, you don't open the shop for hours. Just so you know, *TWO* eggs sound really good for breakfast, don't they?"

Gwen waggled her eyebrows.

Good grief! She's giving me her approval of "candidate number two" in front of him. Violet gave Gwen her best displeased look—deep frown, evil eye, puckered brow, and all.

"Yes, yes." Violet fluttered her hands at her sister. "Go eat. Devon and I won't be long."

Gwen smiled a little too sweetly and waved. "Bye, Mr. Moore. Happy picking."

She turned and marched toward the kitchen with a perkiness to her step.

Violet smiled demurely, her heart fluttering at the idea of being near Devon. "I'll put on my hat, and I'll be ready."

Devon held the door open. "Splendid."

Violet pinned on her hat, and they left.

~

A half hour later, Violet and Devon both bent over rows of ripe, red berries. The hairy underside of the deep-green, scalloped leaves clung to Violet's skin, as if wanting to be chosen as well. She stood up and stretched, looking over at Devon's row. She saw quite a few berries peeking out from the leaves Devon had passed over.

Violet laughed and pointed behind him. "I think you've missed some."

He stood up straight and gazed back at his row.

Shrugging, he told her, "I can't see where they are very well. When I was a child, a doctor discovered that I'm colorblind. Apparently, I mix up green and red colors, but also have trouble discerning dark colors."

Violet shielded her eyes from the late morning sun.

"I've heard of people being colorblind but have never known anyone who is."

Devon winked at her. "Now, you can consider yourself lucky."

In a way Violet did see herself as blessed for knowing Devon, colorblindness aside. "That would be awful for me to manage at my flower shop, having that, but I suppose it doesn't cause you too much grief at your work."

"Not really," Devon admitted before bending over to finish the last few feet of his row.

Violet completed picking her row and compared baskets with Devon.

Devon scratched the side of his head. "If I'm missing some and you're picking more than me, why doesn't it show?"

Blushing, Violet confessed, "I do tend to eat a few as I pick."

With a knowing smile, Devon arched his brows. "A few? I have almost twice as much as you."

A laugh escaped Violet, something that happened much more frequently of late. "I guess you caught me."

Echoing her laugh, Devon reached for her hand. "Let's go, and I'll pay for these."

Violet started to protest over him paying for both baskets, but Devon held up his hand.

"It's my treat," he firmly told her.

She had to admit it felt nice to be treated special. Even if it was only strawberries and not diamonds, but she wouldn't want diamonds anyway. Amethysts or emeralds were more to her taste. "

Thank you," she said.

They walked to the stand on the end of the strawberry field and Devon paid. Violet took his arm. They ambled to a hill covered in prairie grass, with a view of the farm, and sat down, Devon placing their baskets beside them.

Violet tucked her knees up to her chin, her moss-green skirt blending in with their surroundings, and thought how she hadn't done this in years—sit like a girl in the grass. She peered sideways at Devon. He looked younger today. He had on a simple pair of trousers and a plain, tan and blue, plaid shirt, no tie, and no jacket. She liked him better like this, rather than in a suit and tie.

On impulse she asked, "Have you enjoyed being in the lumber business?"

He shrugged. "I didn't have much to say about it. My father expected my brother and I to follow in his footsteps. I can't say that I enjoy it, but it's what I know."

Violet had the sudden urge to confess her previous suspicions to him. He likely had little to do with how his manager acquired trees, and definitely less than no involvement in Roger's death. Still, she tested the water.

"You know, for a while, I wondered whether Moore Lumber had something to do with my husband Roger's death."

With wide eyes and shocked tone, Devon turned to her. "Why would you think that?"

Resting her gaze on her twiddling fingers, Violet told him, "A representative from the company came out last year to our home and was very forceful in his mission to purchase our trees for lumber. He went so far as to send a lumber team to survey our woods, even after we declined his offer."

"I'm sorry to hear that. Did you get a name? If not, I can make some enquiries. But what could that have to do with your husband's death?"

Violet met his concerned eyes, which had an uncharacteristic dimness to them. "Thank you, but actually, Frankie went to the office and asked some questions on my behalf. It seems I was mistaken, for he found nothing to suggest the man would go so far as to come after Roger physically, which was my belief."

Violet moved her hands to the grass, tugging on a few blades.

Devon slid his hand next to hers and did the same, until he curled a few fingers around hers, calming her movement. "I'm glad you found the company not to be involved, but I wish you'd asked me. Instead, Mr. Dermot had to come to your rescue."

His tone held unmistakable afront.

Violet squeezed his fingers. "Frankie didn't *have* to help me. He offered because we're old friends. Besides," she nudged his shoulder with hers, "I didn't know you very well then."

Devon turned fully toward Violet. He reached out his other hand and stroked her jawline with a few fingers. "Is that all Mr. Dermot is to you, an old friend?"

Violet nodded. She blinked and leaned closer to Devon, as he did to her. They shared the same intimate space. He smelled of bergamot and cedar and fresh-picked strawberries. She glanced down at their entwined, red-stained fingers.

He tipped her chin up and touched her lightly on the lips with his, silently asking for more.

Violet leaned in and gave in to his request, their lips meeting over and over again, in gentle, easy kisses.

Devon leaned back. "Oh, Violet."

His words purred out, slow, meaningful.

Violet soaked in his gaze and felt an affection from him that she hadn't expected nor sought, but which made her rejoice. She knew without a doubt that she cared for him.

He gave her one more kiss then stood, reaching for her hand. "Should we head back to town? I can ask Mrs. Porter to make a light lunch for us."

Putting her hand in his, Violet said, "I should head to the shop, but how about you join Gwen and I for a light supper, instead? I have cold cuts for sandwiches, and we can have strawberries for dessert with some leftover sponge cake. After supper, I can show you my greenhouses and gardens."

It pleased Violet greatly to think of showing off her

gardens, her labor of love, to Devon. Inviting him to the home she once shared with Roger did not hit her as wrong. Instead, it felt like a natural step to take.

He pulled her up and smiled, his eyes bright and twinkling again. "I'd like that very much, but I have an appointment this evening. Can we plan for another time?"

Violet deflated. She had hoped he'd say yes, but she smiled and answered, "Most certainly."

Devon picked up both baskets with one hand, and they took their time walking to his buggy and horse, their hands clasped together the whole way. The prairie grass brushed against her skirt and his legs.

Happiness of a kind Violet hadn't experienced in a while spread over her, like the comfort of a warm blanket on a cold day. Oh, growing flowers and her shop made her happy, but it wasn't the same sort of joy. She sent up a prayer of thanks for the kind, handsome man who had walked into Fragrant Sentiments one day and now into her heart.

*Sisters are flowers from
a different garden.*

~

Author unknown

CHAPTER ELEVEN

The next morning, Gwen helped Webster water the gardens while Violet made breakfast—biscuits and sausage gravy. Violet was still dwelling on her hours with Devon yesterday and didn't care for the fact that Gwen had invited Webster to stay and share breakfast with them. Another day, perhaps. Violet would have liked to extend such an invitation to Webster earlier but hadn't, her being a widow living alone. With Gwen here it was more acceptable.

Far from the awkwardness of her encounters with Web of late, breakfast passed in pleasant conversation, and he held his own with Gwen's many questions. Indeed, Violet confirmed again what she had already known—Webster Polinski was a nice young man.

After breakfast, the three of them squeezed into the buggy, and Webster drove Milly to town. Now, he worked on setting up deliveries, and Violet and Gwen went through the opening chore list for the shop. Holly joined them at 8:30, appearing thrilled to meet Violet's sister. They made short work of the opening duties, and Violet unlocked the shop door at 9:00 sharp.

After organizing the enclosure cards, as Violet had asked her to do, Gwen put a hand on her hip. "I wonder if you'll get another one today?"

"Another what?" Holly asked, as she stripped the bottom leaves off a bunch of delphinium, which Webster had cut from the gardens yesterday and had been sitting in a processing solution in the cool room.

Violet chose a blue, glass vase, to echo the blue of the blossoms, off the shelf of vases behind her worktable. "Oh, nothing. Just a late bit of mail."

Keeping her gaze from meeting Gwen's or Holly's, Violet added some water to the vase from a watering can on the worktable.

"A love note, you mean," Holly said.

Violet stopped pouring and looked over at Holly. "How did you know?"

A smile stretched Holly's mouth wide. "I didn't. I guessed, and now I know for sure. What else would fancy, perfumed paper contain?" She stripped another delphinium stem of its leaves. "Did you receive one yesterday, after I left?"

"Yes," Violet confessed.

She added fern fronds and leafy branches she had cut from a forsythia bush a few days ago to the vase in front of her.

Gwen swatted the air with one hand, her other pressed against her bosom. "You should have heard the sender's profession of love."

Lining up the finished delphinium stems, Holly gave them a fresh, even cut with a pair of floral shears, and plunked the flowers into the waiting display bucket before air bubbles could get trapped in the cut end of the stems. "Any idea who it is?"

Before Violet could answer Gwen jumped in.

"We've narrowed it down to three candidates: Webster, Frankie, and Devon," Gwen declared. "My money's on Devon."

Holly tilted her head, wearing a puzzled expression. "My uncle? I can't imagine him doing such a thing. And Web." She shook her head and uttered a firm, "No, definitely not. Who's Frankie?"

Violet added some lupine to her vase. "Remember, I introduced you to Mr. Dermot the other day."

With a nod, Holly said, "Oh, yes. Him I can see."

A giggle bubbled up from Violet. "Really? In my mind he seems the least likely of the three to pen me sweet nothings."

Gwen rolled her eyes. "That's for sure. You should have seen the antics he got up to in school."

Holly picked up the delphinium bucket and encircled it with her arms, snugging it against her side, the flower heads reaching the crown of Holly's head. "On second thought, Violet, you and Uncle Devon would make a lovely pair." She smiled that sweet smile of hers. "He is the devoted type. As far as I know Uncle Devon only ever loved one woman, but perhaps that has changed now."

Violet's ears perked up. "Oh? And who was this woman who so captured your uncle's admiration?"

She fixed her eyes on Holly.

Holly's smile drooped in a sad way, so similar to how Devon smiled on occasion. Her dark eyes flicked up to Violet's.

"My...mother," Holly said before walking the bucket of delphinium to the flower display.

With wide, incredulous eyes, Gwen asked Violet in a voice low enough that Holly wouldn't hear. "Her mother?"

Violet shrugged in response. Holly had never hinted at such a thing, and the fact of it shocked Violet, she had to admit. Clearly, some secret heartbreak nestled in the Moores' past. In a way Violet could sympathize with Devon, but she prayed that neither of them would end up with a broken heart, whether he turned out to be her secret admirer or not. Though pulled toward Devon and remembering their kisses of yesterday, Violet could not be certain as yet that she loved him. It was all so confusing—her three potential admirers.

Holly came back, and Violet asked, "Would you tell us more about what happened with your uncle and your mother? I take it that must have been before you were born."

Gwen chimed in, "Likely two brothers vying for the same woman. An age-old tale."

She sighed and used a dust cloth to dust around some gift items on display. Violet thought it amazing how quickly Gwen had gone from near despondency upon her arrival yesterday to chipper than a chipmunk with her cheeks full of acorns.

Tucking her arms across her chest and leaning on the counter for a minute, Holly answered, "I don't know if I should tell you." She sighed. "But I'd rather you found out from me than some old town gossip. Really, it's astounding that you haven't heard, being from this area—it was quite the scandal." Holly looked directly at Violet. "Do you really want to know?"

Violet nodded, and Gwen piped up, "Sure do."

Rolling her eyes, Violet said to Gwen, "You don't get a say."

Gwen frowned but kept quiet.

Using a hand towel, Holly wiped the leaves that had accumulated on the counter onto the floor, to sweep up later. She faced Violet. "I think his feelings for her did go way back, but when I was ten years old, Uncle Devon tricked us all into thinking he was my father. You see, they were identical twins."

Violet and Gwen gasped in tandem. Imagining kind, quiet Devon to be so devious didn't seem possible to Violet, and he had never mentioned being a twin to her.

"Can you explain more about what exactly happened?" she asked Holly.

Holly went on to tell them of her father's death and how Devon had switched roles with him, pretending that he had died and that he was William, Holly's father.

"It was long ago, so don't think too harshly of him," Holly begged Violet.

It was all too much to take in for Violet.

Thankfully, the shop began to get busy with customers, for Violet didn't know how to respond to Holly and what she had revealed. Holly obviously loved her uncle and must have buried the past grievances he had cost her, but it revealed something to Violet—in Devon lay a heart of deception. And she would not entertain thoughts of a man's company when he carried such a dishonest mark.

But those kisses. Surely, they were true.

No! He's nothing better than another trap-setter, like the man who set a trap for Roger, her protective heart told her.

Maybe that was too harsh, but honesty was of paramount importance to Violet. She knew she shouldn't judge someone by their past sins, but heaven help her, she couldn't rise above it. Not judging others had always been difficult for her, a besetting fault. And after reaching forty, she ought to know herself well enough to recognize that. But could she overlook it, let it go? Devon had never mentioned a word of it to her, and perhaps if he had…

But when could he have? One did not interject such things into a polite conversation. Violet mulled the whole issue over in her mind while she worked.

The morning passed, busy and with no opportunity to pick up their previous thread of conversation. At noon Holly said her goodbyes, in a more reserved way than usual. Her warm, bubbly aura had disappeared, and that saddened Violet.

Web finished early and left for the day too. Frankie came into the shop a half hour before closing, and his presence cheered Violet considerably.

His sturdy, tall physique moved toward Violet's worktable. He smiled, all straight teeth and bright eyes. Wearing his hair slicked back, a tight collar around his neck with a lapis-blue, silk tie, and a well-fitting, charcoal suit, Frankie looked like a successful man.

He pulled out a paper from the leather satchel he carried. "I'm happy to catch you. I have some news."

Gwen sashayed toward them from her job of putting the flowers on display back in the cool room. "Well, as I live and breathe. Dodgy Dermot."

She cracked a wide smile.

Frankie laughed. "Haven't heard that name in a good while. Hello, Gwen. How's life treating you?"

Angling her head and spearing him with one pale green eye, Gwen said, "Recognized me straight away, huh?"

"Sure did. I'd know you anywhere. You and Violet look so much alike."

Gwen sent him a saucy wink. "Except I'm prettier."

He cleared his throat. "That is if you prefer fair beauty. Now I have always had an eye for a dark-haired lass."

Frankie's eyes shifted to Violet's. Violet wanted to trust his words, but she couldn't be sure they rang true.

She offered Frankie a brief smile but then turned to Gwen. "Franklin and I have some business to discuss. Would you mind giving us some privacy?"

She hated to sound so formal, but Gwen had the tendency to stick her nose where it didn't belong. And better to be clear with her from the start.

Lifting her brows, Gwen said, "If that's what you wish." She nodded to Frankie. "Nice to see you."

Frankie jerked his head. "You as well."

When Gwen had turned and left them, Violet asked Frankie, "What have you found?"

Focusing on her vow to unearth Roger's killer would take Violet's mind off Devon and the startling revelation she had learned of. She took the paper he held out to her and glanced at it.

He explained, "The mercantile owner, Mr. Conley, received a letter from his niece. I wrote down what he told me she remembered about the man who bought a trap that day in May. A younger man. With light hair and eyes. Normal build. That's all she said she could recall, so I'm going to cross-check that with the Moore surveyors and managers list I created previously. I didn't find anything when I questioned them before, but now we have a description, I'll see if anyone matches it and try again." He lifted his pocket watch out of his vest pocket and looked at it. "I better be off. Can't stay, but how about we plan another meal date to talk over my findings? What do you say to supper this time at The Paul House?"

Violet handed him back the paper. "That would be lovely."

"Pick you up here at 6:00 in the evening tomorrow?" he asked, his deep voice smooth and enticing.

Then Violet remembered her sister. She didn't know if Gwen was staying through to Sunday. "I have to check with Gwen and see when she's leaving."

He shoved the paper back in his satchel. "Sure, but I leave the day after tomorrow."

"So soon?"

Violet didn't want Frankie to go. She enjoyed his company and their shared scheme.

"Yes, I must go. But I'll stop by tomorrow." Smiling, he turned to leave, all business again.

"Thanks for all your help," Violet told him.

"Anytime."

He walked to the door, waved, and slipped out.

Gwen appeared a second later, wearing her lips in a firm line. "So, you've some dealings with Frankie, huh?"

Violet didn't elaborate. "Yes."

"I wouldn't trust him, if I were you."

Violet wiped the surface of the worktable. "Well,

good thing I'm not you."

In the serious sisterly tone Violet remembered, Gwen said, "Whatever it is you're involved with, be careful. That's all I'm saying."

"Ha! Famous last words."

Violet smirked at Gwen, and they both chuckled. It hit Violet's funny bone because Gwen always had something to say. And the idea that she would stop asking Violet about Frankie was ridiculous.

Sure feels good to laugh. Violet rejoiced that Gwen had come to visit. The last few days had done them both good.

Reining in her mirth, Violet turned serious. "When do you have to leave?"

Gwen swept around the design area. "Figured that I'd take the Sunday afternoon train."

"I'll be sorry to see you go." Violet reached out to Gwen, and Gwen hugged her with one arm. "We've talked more about my life than yours."

They let each other go.

Gwen resumed a slow, steady sweeping. "And it was exactly what I needed." She tipped her gaze up. "And next time, you're coming to visit me."

"I will," Violet agreed.

"Promise?" Gwen leaned on the handle of the broom for a few seconds.

"Let's plan it now." Violet slipped off her apron and hung it on a nearby hook then took out the small monthly planner she kept by her design station. She flipped to the end of June and scanned through July. "I'm fairly free after Holly's wedding at the end of June." She looked at Gwen. "Would you care for a guest over the Fourth of July?"

"That would be wonderful," Gwen exclaimed, and the sisters chatted about what they would do over the holiday.

It pleased Violet that only a faint ache remained in her heart over Devon. It certainly would do her good to get away and obtain a fresh perspective on the scope of secret admirers and Fragrant Sentiments.

Webster met them at the shop as Violet locked up. "May I escort you ladies home?"

It eased Violet's mind not to have to hitch Milly up and drive home. "Yes, thank you. That's so kind, Web."

She flashed him a tired smile.

"I'll go get Milly and pick you up."

Webster didn't wait for an answer but trotted toward the livery. Violet and Gwen sat and waited on a bench outside the shop.

Gwen leaned back on the bench and stretched her legs out. "Sure is a handy young man."

"Yes," Violet agreed and thought about how well she and Webster worked together.

What if? Violet entertained the thought, though, yet again, Web's age stood like a brick wall between them. *But walls can be broken down, busted through. Can't they?*

Perhaps, but the fortitude to tackle such a barrier did

not exist in Violet at the moment, and her feelings rested heavily in Devon's camp. She didn't want to entertain the possibility of Webster playing the role of her secret admirer. For now, she needed to focus her mind and energy on the vow still burning in her heart. Once she'd seen Roger had justice, there'd be time enough for love then.

Never seek to tell thy love
Love that never told can be.

William Blake

CHAPTER TWELVE

Early Sunday afternoon, Violet embraced her sister, and for a few moments she didn't want to let go. Rarely the type of person to revel in or seek physical touch, Violet soaked up the love Gwen had shown her during her visit, realizing how much Gwen had blessed her by visiting. The pressure of Gwen's hands on Violet's back eased, and they drew apart.

Gwen narrowed her eyes, but her lips were relaxed. "Remember now, I expect to see you over the Fourth. I'll come and drag you to our place myself if I have to."

"Yes, I know. I promise I'll come." Reaching into the basket on her arm, Violet pulled out a corsage of two small, purple irises she had made for Gwen. She pinned it on Gwen's traveling jacket, at the shoulder.

"To remember our time, as irises are for remembrance."

With one finger Gwen touched the soft, purple petals. She looked up at Violet, her eyes watering. "Thanks, Vi. You write to me if anything new develops in the secret admirer department."

Violet nodded.

"Aye, aye, captain," she kidded with a mock salute.

"I'm serious." Gwen playfully swatted Violet's arm and winked. "I still think your best bet is Dashing Devon."

"Is that what you're calling him now?" Violet asked.

In the few days that Gwen had stayed with Violet and discovered her secret, she'd applied a revolving door of nicknames to the men they had both deemed candidates for the role of Violet's secret admirer.

"All aboard," the conductor called out as he strolled along the edge of the train station platform.

A young man and woman rushed past. Several other people slipped by Violet and Gwen. The train released a burst of steam, and Gwen lifted her bag, stepping up into the train.

She turned. "Give my regards to Winsome Webster. I didn't see him this morning before we left. Oh, and Holly. I'm sure the wedding will be lovely. You must tell me all about it when you come."

Winsome? Violet supposed that adjective fit Web well, him being an all-around likable fellow.

She raised her voice to be heard over the bustle of activity and the sounds of the train. "I will."

A few more passengers got on the train before it belched forth more steam and started to roll forward.

Gwen waved. "All right then."

Violet raised her arm and waved back, watching until Gwen ducked into the car, and her heart ached a little. She had never enjoyed a visit with Gwen more.

Back to business, Violet reminded herself. Running late to meet Holly at the shop, Violet didn't stay to see the train steam out of sight. With a brisk pace, Violet headed back to the buggy and drove Milly to the livery. After leaving Milly in capable hands, she hurried to Fragrant Sentiments. Upon unlocking the door and entering, Violet saw Holly perched at the worktable. *She must have let herself in with her spare key.*

Violet walked back to her worktable to start on the enjoyable task of going over Holly's wedding arrangements with her one more time on paper. The roses Violet had ordered would come in early next week, just a few days before the wedding. She worried the heads might be too closed but hoped for the best.

Holly lifted her head and stopped flipping through a magazine. "Did Gwen get off without any trouble?"

Violet seated herself on the other stool and opened her wedding planning album atop the table. "Oh, yes. She said to say goodbye."

She paged to where she had the details of Holly's wedding.

Holly placed a rolled-up paper on the table between them. "Have you seen this?"

She pointed to an editorial piece on the second page of the daily newspaper.

Turning the paper to read it, Violet scanned that section and gasped when she realized it was about her shop. She glanced up and caught Holly's eye.

Holly shook her head. "I know, it's terrible. It seems 'Stanley Bear' has a grievance with us."

Violet read the worst sentence aloud. "*I have never been treated so rudely or experienced such incompetent service.*"

In short, the brief paragraph had maligned the shop and its service without naming any names, but what other flower shop was in the area? None.

Reaching out her hand, Holly patted Violet's hand on the table. "A pack of lies. Think nothing of it."

Violet's tummy sank, giving her that dead-weight sensation in her gut. She should have known Mr. Clemmons would be the type to seek retribution.

She groaned. "Actually, it's fairly close to the truth. I did refuse him service, and I suppose it was our fault that we got the messages mixed up."

Violet leaned back in her chair.

Holly pouted, lowering her sad eyes. "You mean *I* got them mixed up."

Violet rushed to reassure Holly. "I'm not blaming you. It was an accident. He's the one at fault. He should have sealed the envelopes and attached them to the bouquets." Violet heaved out a sigh. "Well, we'll just have to weather whatever comes of it. There's nothing else to do."

"I'm sure your loyal customers will see past this," Holly pointed out.

"Perhaps."

Violet had her doubts. People were fickle.

Holly brightened with a smile. "Maybe you should run a sale. Nothing helps people forget more than a bargain, I'd wager."

"That's a good idea. We'll put that in the works for tomorrow, and maybe I will advertise it in the paper."

Violet's gut unclenched and a wave of relief rolled over her. Looking back, she wouldn't have handled the situation with Mr. Clemmons any differently. She'd gone with her conscience, come what may. She breathed a prayer. *Lord, help this not be a permanent mark on my business.* She'd leave her reputation in God's hands. He'd be better at looking after it than she was.

Pushing the newspaper aside, Violet told Holly, "Let's move on to why we are both here."

Holly smiled. "Agreed. I didn't think you'd mind, so I asked Matthew to join us. You've not met him yet, and I thought this would be the perfect opportunity." Holly glanced at the clock on the wall. "He should be here shortly. We came separately as he had something to check on at the lumberyard."

"Certainly. But what brings him to the lumber company on a Sunday? Aren't they closed?" Violet asked.

A slight twinge of annoyance picked at Violet. She'd

wanted to talk with Holly alone and ask her more about Devon and the terrible trick he had played on Holly and her family.

Holly hiked one shoulder up. "He just told me he needed something he had left at the office."

At that moment Violet heard what sounded like knocking. "Is he at the front door?"

She leaned and looked that way. Sure enough, a man in a tan suit and hat stood outside knocking on the glass door.

Jumping off her stool, Holly said, "I'll let him in."

Violet sighed and laid aside her plan of having a more intimate conversation with Holly. Maybe what she should be doing was asking Devon herself, but she didn't have the courage to, at least not right now.

Holly came back with a handsome young man in tow. He took off his hat and smiled. She introduced Violet, and Violet liked Matthew Peterson immediately. With gentle, hazel eyes behind a set of spectacles, soft-looking, sandy hair, and an easy smile, Matthew seemed a good match for Holly.

Violet slipped off her stool. "Let's go sit at the table by the plants. There's more seating there."

She led the way, carrying her album, and after taking their seats, she started in.

Violet went over all the arrangements, and the intended couple did little else but nod, smile, and even giggle a few times when they exchanged meaningful glances, full of such adoration.

Did Roger ever look at me like that? Violet couldn't recall. She had known Roger loved her, but not like this young man, who was so obviously smitten with Holly. A strange desire to be the object of someone's abandoned affection grew in Violet. And perhaps the hope of such a thing was still possible and not past the scope of comprehension, at least according to the love notes she'd been receiving.

Violet closed the album. "I look forward to creating these arrangements and bouquets to complement what I am sure will be a very special day."

"It's going to be so beautiful." Holly curved her well-proportioned lips back and lifted her eyes to Matthew's.

He smiled back just as sweetly. "Yes, it will, my love."

He brushed the top of her hand with his thumb.

But Holly's smile suddenly fell, and she looked at Violet with wide eyes. "Are you sure you won't need help with the bouquets? I could…"

Violet could read Holly's thoughts and held a hand up and stopped her. "Absolutely not." She shook her head and placed her hand firmly on the table. "You will have other more important details to see to."

Matthew glanced at Violet first then focused on Holly. He clasped both his hands around hers. "Mrs. Brooks is right. We'll need those few days before the wedding to get everything in order."

Holly slipped her hands out from his, and they curled their fingertips around each other's. "I suppose you're right." She turned to Violet, hope in her eyes. "And you will come to the wedding, right? I mean, not just as our florist or my employer but as a friend."

"Of course," Violet said.

"I know that Uncle Devon would be very pleased to see you there."

"Would he?" Violet squeaked out.

She hadn't meant to ask that aloud. *When will I ever learn to think before I speak?*

"Oh, of course." An unmistakable twinkle glittered in Holly's eyes. "He thinks very highly of you and is often commenting on what an interesting and lovely lady you are."

Heat rushed up Violet's back and bloomed on her cheeks at the thought of Devon's compliments. She suppressed her thoughts of him.

"I will most assuredly attend as your guest," she simply told Holly, not mentioning Devon again.

"Good." Holly paused and tilted her head, narrowing one eye. "I had been thinking but didn't mention that I…" Her gaze flicked to Matthew. "Um…"

She started coughing. Matthew patted her on the back, but she continued.

"Are you all right?" he asked Holly.

"I think," *cough,* "I may need…" *more coughing,* "a glass of water."

Holly pointed and rolled her wrist at the pitcher of water and several glasses Violet always kept waiting on a stand in her office area.

He jumped up from his seat, attentively. "Yes, I'll be right back."

With a brisk step, he crossed the room.

As soon as he was out of earshot, Holly stopped coughing, leaned across the table, and whispered, "I think Uncle Devon may be your secret admirer."

An instant fluttering beat in Violet's chest at Holly's words. "Why would you think so?"

"I saw him writing a note on paper that looked an awful lot like the notes you've been receiving." Glancing in Matthew's direction, Holly spoke quickly, her words clumped together. "Do you like him? Would you return his affection? You would make a lovely couple. Oh, I do hope so," she pleaded, her eyes as wide as a child's on Christmas morning.

Violet saw Matthew walking back and hurried into speech. "Mr. Moore is a most pleasant man, and at one time I would not have objected but…"

Violet held on to her words, worrying about how to tactfully address the Moore skeletons in the closet.

Matthew approached and set the glass of water he had poured in front of Holly. "And here we are; this should help."

He flashed a slightly lopsided grin at Holly then sat down.

"Thanks." Holly smiled back and took a gulp of water. "All better now."

Placing a light kiss on Holly's cheek, Matthew said, "Good." He turned to look at the clock on the wall.

"Well, we should be going, Holly. I need to get back. Father wanted to discuss something with me."

Holly's bottom lip drooped. "On your day off?"

"It won't take long." He moved to rise. "Thank you, Mrs. Brooks, for all of your help. I'm sure the flowers will be beautiful."

Standing now, he held out a hand to Holly.

She took his hand but protested, "But there were still a few details we didn't discuss, and…"

"I believe we covered everything about the wedding." Violet smiled and stood, relieved that Matthew had unknowingly derailed Violet's reply to Holly's questions. "And I'll see you both next week."

Violet hoped Holly would drop her inquiries, with much more important details to occupy her mind.

Holly finally stood, despite the shadow on her brow, and they all walked toward the door. "Yes, see you then." Leaning forward to embrace Violet, Holly whispered into her ear, "Trust me. He's the one."

"Perhaps," Violet whispered back, returning her hug.

She didn't want to encourage Holly's belief that Devon was her secret admirer. They broke apart, Matthew slightly tugging on Holly's arm.

"Thank you again," he said as he opened the door, looking oblivious to how Holly held back.

He began to step over the threshold. Reaching out, Violet clung to the door and held it open wide for them.

"You'll think about what I said?" Holly asked, her

eyes trained on Violet.

Violet dropped her gaze momentarily and avoided Holly's question. "Have a pleasant afternoon, and I'll see you soon."

Flicking her gaze back up to Holly, Violet cracked a slight smile.

"Thank you," Matthew called a last time, and he commandeered Holly along.

"Yes, yes...see you at the wedding..." Holly craned her head back and waved.

Violet fluttered her fingers and closed and locked the door as soon as Holly's heel cleared the step, chiding herself for acting foolishly. She supposed it was only natural for Holly to place Devon in the role of secret admirer. He was her uncle, after all.

Maybe Violet had not given Devon enough credit. She certainly hadn't granted him an opportunity to explain himself. As she moved around her shop checking on displays, straightening the enclosure cards, fluffing the silk flowers displayed in painted, ceramic urns, and picking a few yellow leaves off the green plants sheltering the table and chairs in the consultation area, Violet turned her mind toward prayer.

She hadn't prayed enough about her secret admirer dilemma nor her attempt at finding justice for Roger. Moving forward in her own strength, Violet realized she had not laid her burdens at the foot of the cross, where they needed to be.

With the dead leaves clutched in her hand that she

had picked off the plants, Violet made her way to the design area to toss them into the garbage. She threw the leaves away and brushed her hands together.

A prayer rose in her heart and on her lips. "Lord, I don't know what I'm doing. I'm flattered by the attention I'm receiving but don't know if I am ready to have another man in my life. Help me to know. And help me remember that vengeance is yours to mete out, not mine. If some justice has yet to be found for Roger, would you uncover it? If not, help me to…let it go."

As her words came to an end, Violet marveled at how refreshed her spirit was. It amazed her that a simple, heartfelt prayer could ease her mind.

"Thank you," she uttered as a kind of amen.

She rinsed her hands at the sink and dried them on a nearby towel, then jumped at the *thump, thump, thump* she heard. She placed a hand over her heart, trying to calm her pumping organ. Hurrying toward the front door, she glimpsed Frankie through the glass. He grinned at her and tipped his hat.

Violet smiled at the sight of her friend and investigative partner. She'd forgotten Frankie had said he would stop by.

She turned the lock on the door and let him in, locking it again behind him. "I almost forgot you were meeting me."

Frankie removed his hat, the slight bald spot on his head shining in the sunlight slanting through the windows.

He pouted in an exaggerated fashion. "You wound me, Vi. Am I so easily forgotten?"

"Of course not." Violet met his steady gaze with a sure eye and a tone of voice that she hoped conveyed her fondness for him. "How is your afternoon?"

His features reverted to his usual relaxed lips and brows. "Good, good." He flashed a well-formed grin at her. "All the better for seeing you."

Statements like these drove Frankie higher on the list of her possible admirers, but Violet brushed off the compliment.

She swatted the air with a hand and lightly laughed. "Go on with you."

He stepped closer, close enough for Violet to smell a hint of spice and clove.

Cupping her elbow in his hand, Frankie asked, "How about I take you for a drive? It's a lovely afternoon, and you shouldn't be cooped up here in the shop."

"That does sound nice. I don't usually work on Sunday, but it was the only time I could meet Holly and her fiancé to discuss the final wedding details. I'll accompany you. Just let me shut the lights off and collect my hat and bag."

"Need any help?"

"I can manage."

Violet hurried to the back, pushed the switch to shut off the electric lights in the rear end of the store, caught up her favorite purple hat from the stand by her office area, and collected her crocheted bag off her desk. She flitted to Frankie's side and stopped to fix her hat to her head with an abalone-tipped hatpin, crested with her initials. Roger had given it to her for their first wedding anniversary. *Roger.* Would she ever stop missing him? His crooked smile, the way he guffawed at a joke, and his attention to detail, making the simplest flower a thing of beauty in one of his designs.

"Ready?" Frankie asked, peering down at her.

Violet nodded. "Lead the way."

Frankie opened the front show door and stepped out. Violet followed, locking the door behind them. She took Frankie's offered elbow, and they walked to his waiting horse and carriage a few feet down the road.

When they were both settled inside and Frankie had directed his horse, Sam, onward, Violet started the conversation.

"I suppose there's no chance you found anything new. Any lead on the lumber company?"

"Nah, didn't turn up anything else. No one matched the description at the company. Sorry, Vi." He shrugged his large shoulders. "There may be nothing to turn up."

A ragged sigh rushed out of Violet. Frustrated, she exclaimed, "I don't know how that can be. Someone is responsible for placing that trap in the woods, and if it isn't the lumber company, who can it be?"

"Your guess is as good as mine. I double checked with all your neighbors. They all claim to be innocent of any involvement. Are you sure Roger didn't have any enemies?"

Violet laughed loudly. "You wouldn't ask that if you had known Roger."

He didn't comment, and neither did she. Irritation bubbled up in Violet but then a thought. *It's time to release your vow.*

Whether it was her own conscience or God's spirit, she couldn't tell. She let her thoughts drift with the rattle and bump of the wheels on the road.

After several minutes of quiet, Frankie spoke up. "I leave for Chicago tomorrow morning."

Violet set aside her own agenda and turned to Frankie with what she hoped was an expression of fondness. "I'll miss you."

Frankie returned her gaze, a soft, welcoming look in his eye. "And I'll miss you. I thoroughly enjoyed our little adventure, although it led to a dead end." He cleared his throat. "With my mother growing older, I've considered moving…back to Chippewa Falls."

Shocked, Violet sucked in a breath. "And give up your job at the paper? What would you do here?"

"Perhaps start my own paper or write remotely for a while, submitting articles to various papers. But…"

Frankie slowed his horse and pulled him to a stop under the largest elm tree Violet had ever seen. She looked around and realized they were east of town by the park.

He finished, "I'd have to be certain there was more

to come home to than just a job." He let go of the reins and with a slow, soft movement collected Violet's hand in his. "Would you welcome my further attention?"

Swallowing a lump, Violet couldn't say for sure. She did like Frankie and enjoyed his company very much, but she didn't want him to uproot his life for her. Especially since she didn't love him, not yet. *There it is—I don't love him.* Maybe in time. But was that what she desired—an uncertain relationship which might or might not lead to love?

Violet wanted something different than she had enjoyed with Roger. She'd heard other friends and Gwen talk about their romantic flutterings and the feeling of being swept away by desire. Violet really wanted the man who'd written her the notes.

"I'm sorry, Frankie, but I can't give you a sure answer." She squeezed his strong fingers. She rolled her thumb over a lump on his middle finger, likely from writing. "Right now, you are my friend. All I can give you is a maybe that I might feel more deeply with time."

He bit his bottom lip and nodded in a resigned way. "I figured as much, but I had to ask. You probably wouldn't have guessed, but I lost my heart to you in primary school."

His sad eyes weighed on Violet's heart. She'd had no idea he had held feelings for her for so long.

"And then you married Roger, and I moved away." He dropped her hand.

"We can write," Violet weakly offered.

"We're too old for maybes, Vi."

She laughed. "Who are you calling old?"

He echoed her and laughed too. "Poor choice of words." Frankie gathered the reins and urged his horse on, his usual cheerful spirit back. "Let's finish our ride. Mom wanted me to ask if you'd join us for supper."

Violet breathed easier, grateful the intensity between them had passed. "I'd like that very much."

"It'll make her happy. She's been pestering me for days to ask you."

Violet rested her hand lightly on Frankie's dark blue suit jacket. "Then I won't disappoint her."

They visited and chatted companionably on the mile back to Frankie's mother's home, and Violet felt settled in her spirit that she'd finally defined her feelings for her long-ago beau.

I hide myself within my flower,
that, fading from your vase,
you, unsuspecting feel for me,
almost a loneliness.

Emily Dickinson

CHAPTER THIRTEEN

The next day, Violet and Frankie rode to the train station together for her to see him off.

Violet let her gaze rove over her old schoolmate. "I'm so glad we renewed our friendship, Frankie. I'll miss you. I wish you could stay longer."

Frankie collected her hands and cradled them in his. "And you're sure that's all we share—a friendship?"

His eyes searched hers.

Gulping and nodding, Violet held his penetrating gaze. "I'm very fond of you. That's all I can say for certain for now."

He pulled Violet into a loose embrace and whispered

next to her ear, "I'll take whatever you can offer me, Vi."

He placed a quick kiss on her cheek. Then he let her go.

Violet stood still, rather stupefied, her heart a jumble with too many feelings at once. *Am I sure Frankie is just a friend?* Frankie had proven he really cared about her with the time he'd put into their investigation. That kind of devotion was rare, something that shouldn't be passed up.

But there's Devon. Could she overcome her distaste for his past and let the feelings of love calling to her spring fully forth? That remained to be seen. If Devon hadn't been in her life, Violet could easily have seen herself falling for Frankie. Not in the way she had for Devon, but still falling.

Violet called as Frankie turned away. "Promise to write to me!"

He nodded, smiled, and waved. "I will."

Then he was gone. Violet turned for home with a heavy heart, but in her similitude to Gwen, she couldn't help thinking, *There goes candidate number three.*

Instead of going straight back to the shop, Violet settled Milly at the livery and walked to the park to eat her lunch. She plunked down on a bench under a shady tree and ate her cheese, apple, and most of her bread.

The Chippewa River rolled by, unperturbed by Violet's romantic entanglements or de-tanglements. She stood by the bank and tossed breadcrumbs to the flock of ducks that paddled in a flotilla near the shallows. A slight breeze tickled the corkscrew curls of hair dangling by each of her earlobes.

She hoped being at the park would help get her mind off weddings and flowers, which all spoke of love. She needed a break from the whole theme. The perfect blend of breeze, sun, and moderate temperature made the day a gorgeous one.

People should be happy on days like this.

But Violet couldn't manufacture what wasn't there. She missed Devon, and a most unhappy ache wedged in her middle over the dead end of Roger's case. Deep inside, Violet heard that whispered plea to let go of her vow for justice, and she tried to, but she found it to be more difficult than she had imagined.

Throwing her last crumbs to the ducks, she brushed her hands together and turned to head back to the shop, but a voice stopped her.

"Violet, how lovely to see you. It has been quite a few days since I've had the pleasure of your company."

Violet looked up and focused on…*Devon*. Just the man she didn't want to meet.

"It has," she simply agreed.

She looked him hard in the eyes then swept her gaze to the grass, wondering if her tone sounded as stilted as she felt.

He cleared his throat. In the pause afterwards, Violet let her gaze tip back to his. She couldn't resist.

His left eye pinched at the corner. "Only a few more days until Holly's wedding. Grapevine Lodge has been all aflutter with activity. Are you missing Holly at work?"

It had hit Violet, once Holly had bowed out of work for her prearranged time off for her wedding, how much she had grown to depend on her new, efficient employee. The days had been busy ones before Holly had gone, and she and Violet had not talked further about what Devon had done in years past. In fact, Holly, by all appearances, had forgotten about it. And perhaps Violet should have, too, but she held onto that point of contention. Though she knew keeping a grudge only led to bitterness, she had a difficult time releasing this particular one.

Violet suddenly realized she hadn't answered his question. "Yes, I certainly do." She offered him a slight smile. "I look forward to her return."

Adjusting his tie and shifting his hat on his head, Devon hesitantly moved closer to Violet. She ignored the urge to move away.

"Might I have the honor of escorting you to the wedding, as our...special guest?"

He blinked his clear, blue eyes, an expectant light brightening his face. His salt and brown pepper, closely cropped mustache and beard contoured his face, reminding Violet again how handsome Devon was.

And those eyes. They bored into her. Violet swallowed, her throat feeling dry.

She lowered her gaze from his crystal-blue irises. "It will be such a busy day, and I'll be in and out. I'm sure you'll have other things on your mind than accompanying me."

Not able to keep her eyes off him for long, Violet glanced up again, to see his reaction to her words.

Wrinkles formed above his eyebrows. "Not at all. Holly would want you to enjoy yourself. Can't your arrangements be set up ahead of time?"

He isn't making this easy! Violet inwardly groaned. She had to be honest with him, well, partially honest.

"Really, you are best left free to attend to your guests."

Devon grimaced and scratched at his temple. "Of which you are one."

Violet nodded and clutched her fingers together. Her conscience pricked her over the hurt tone in his voice. "I will be perfectly fine on my own."

She swallowed and braved looking straight at him.

He blinked several times and reached out a hand, slowly as if taming a wild animal, his voice soft. "Violet, if I've done anything to offend you or…have been too forward, I apologize."

Sniffing, Violet slid her gaze away from him and shook her head, attempting to hold back her emotions with a stiff front. "No need. Now, you must excuse me. I have an appointment at 1:30 that I need to prepare for. Good afternoon."

Before she lost her nerve, Violet slipped by him without making eye contact. He didn't call after her or try to stop her, which relieved Violet. She did not consider herself ready to hash over the details of Devon's sordid past.

Still, her heart ached, and she brushed a stray tear off her cheek as she strode back to Fragrant Sentiments.

Violet had really taken to Devon. In addition to him being handsome, she liked how gentle, soft-spoken, sincere, loyal, and loving he was and how alike they were in so many ways. And, of course, he was rich, but that didn't matter to Violet. In fact, his wealth made her nervous, and Violet wished Devon were not quite so well-off.

Another point of connection had been faith. Devon had mentioned his faith to her a number of times. That was important to Violet as well. Her faith in God had gotten her through many trying times and had given her a purpose beyond the work of her hands. Really, Devon represented an almost perfect companion, and if she dared think it, a potential spouse, except for his capability for deception.

"Grrr," Violet growled out loud in frustration, clenching her fists as she stomped the last few feet to the front door of the shop.

Why does he have to be so darn likable! She sucked in a breath, closed her eyes, and tried to compose herself before unlocking the door.

Opening it, she went to step across the threshold when something caught her eye.

"Not now," Violet groaned.

She bent over and picked up another note. It felt

thicker, heavier to her than the previous ones she had received. Whoever had left it must have done so while she was on her lunch break by the river. Frankie was gone and couldn't have, but Devon might have had the time to slip it into the shop and head down to the park. And Web…

"Whatcha got there?"

Webster's familiar voice came from the back of the shop, and she spied him, leaning on the counter, likely working on recording the deliveries before he headed back home.

Tucking the note behind her back, Violet said, "Oh, nothing of importance."

He hitched an eyebrow up. "If you say so."

Clearly, he wasn't convinced. Then Violet thought maybe she should ask Webster about the note and if he saw who had left it. Perhaps she could discover something or trip him up. Violet lowered her arm to her side, revealing the note in her hand.

She showed it to him but kept it out of reach. "This must have been slipped through the letterbox. Did you happen to see anyone around who may have left it?"

He curled his bottom lip down. "Can't say that I have." He scratched at his temple. "Well, come to think of it, there was a fella tinkering around in front of the store. Walked back and forth a few times, then left."

He shrugged a shoulder, girded with a denim overall strap.

"Did you recognize him?"

"Nah, all I saw was a hat and a profile. He stayed in the shade of the awning."

Violet persisted, "What kind of profile? Long nose? A beard?"

"Golly, I don't know, Violet. Like I said, he was in the shadows."

Violet took a deep breath. "Sure. Fine. Sorry, I...well, it's been bothering me for some time."

Webster tilted his head and scrunched his features. "Why? I don't understand."

A sigh escaped Violet. "No, I don't suppose you do." She reached out a hand and brushed his arm. "It's nothing."

In that instant, Violet almost asked Webster outright if he had left the notes for her, but what a fool she would look if he hadn't. And most likely he hadn't.

"Well, all right, but if it's something I can help you with, you should ask." He narrowed his eyes and looked almost mean. "No one is pestering you, are they?"

Violet shook her head. "Oh, no. It's nothing like that."

His voice dipped lower, almost sultry. "Could be someone's sweet on you."

Heat which surely signified a deep blush burned her cheeks. How her body could react so quickly to a few harmless words annoyed Violet greatly.

She hemmed and hawed. "Oh...I'm not...that is to say..." Sweat dampened the back of her neck. Sighing heavily, Violet sputtered, "Yes, they are notes of a romantic inclination."

She chanced a glance at him.

"And you don't know who it is?" he asked, a huge grin on his face, transforming him into a boy again.

A thick patch of his blond hair half covered one eye. Shaking her head, Violet laid the note on the counter.

Webster reached out and swiveled it around to face him. He bent over, closer to the envelope. "Do you recognize the handwriting?"

Violet couldn't say that she could. She'd seen all three of the candidates' penmanship, and none was an exact match. "No."

"Any other clues?" he asked.

Violet couldn't believe she was discussing her secret admirer with Webster. "Well, I'd have to say he's well-spoken, intelligent, versed in the language of flowers, romantic but perhaps shy."

Webster chuckled. "Sounds like quite the dandy."

So it's not Web.

"Oh, I don't know about that." Violet spilled out the truth. "Whoever he is, he's stolen a piece of my heart," she admitted, with regret at not having kept her inner thoughts to herself, yet again.

Without a pause Webster said, "Then he's a lucky man."

Violet placed a cool hand to one of her hot cheeks and changed the subject. "I think I better leave you to finish your work, while I complete the orders for tomorrow."

Nodding and rolling his upper lip, Webster said,

"Sure." He held her gaze a few seconds then lowered his eyes. "I'm almost done."

He plucked a stubby pencil from behind his ear and scratched away at the paper in front of him on the counter, keeping focused on his task.

Violet dragged her feet to her desk and flopped her body down in her chair, which squeaked in protest. She fit her silver letter opener into a gap in the envelope and broke the seal. As she opened the note, a light scent of jasmine perfumed the air. A petite parcel wrapped in brown paper fell from the note onto her desk. Violet carefully opened it and revealed tiny, round, dried, green balls—jasmine tea pearls, Violet guessed. She sought an explanation in the note and read, *"You have touched a part of my soul and opened up my heart. I am yours."* Violet thought the gift and sentiment well-matched. She had read somewhere that in the Orient, people believed jasmine held almost magical powers to open up the soul. She inhaled deeply and closed her eyes, imagining herself seated under the bower of a thick vine of jasmine in a lush garden somewhere in Asia, a faceless man pleading before her.

Who is this imaginary man bowing at my feet? Violet squeezed her eyes shut tight and tried to picture the possible candidates in turn, but none of them fit. More and more, Violet's admirer appeared to be more fiction than fact.

A thudding sound made Violet open her eyes and disentangle herself from her fantasy.

Webster loped toward her desk, wearing his usual, easy-going grin. "That's it for today." He paused, and the skin around his left eye flinched. "Got some errands to run in town for my mother, but I'll stop back at the shop when you close to give you a ride home."

The steady way he looked at her made Violet see Webster in a different light. She had not seen this confident side of him before. Her inclination was to refuse, but she had not driven her mare to town that morning. She had walked, and she didn't relish the thought of the walk home.

"That'd be nice. Thank you," Violet told him.

Nodding, one side of his mouth pulled back, Webster said, "Good. See you then."

Turning, he sauntered out of the shop, whistling a merry tune Violet didn't recognize.

'Here deathless love and passion sleep,'
he cried, 'embodied in this flower.
This is the emblem I will keep.'
Love wore carnations from that hour.

Ella Wheeler Wilcox

CHAPTER FOURTEEN

Violet carefully slid her index finger between the petals of the pink rose in her hand, to coax them open wider. She brought the rose up to her mouth and with a forceful breath of air blew the petals open even more. Satisfied, she gave the stem a fresh, angled cut with her knife and positioned the rose next to another in a large vase of Holly's wedding flowers to create a trio of pink roses above a base of greens, jasmine vines, and two huge heads of blush pink peonies.

The vase stood on a tall stand near where the wedding breakfast would be served and was the last arrangement Violet had to create. Next, she added late-flowering, red tulips, splayed out to the side in graceful arches, then a tiered cluster of red carnations and a few more pink roses; she finished with tall, thick-bladed swamp grass, adding height.

Violet whisked her stem scraps into a basket. Servers bustled about laying out a spread of food fit for a king's banquet table. Looking at her watch, Violet saw that she would need to hurry to get seated in the garden before the ceremony began in ten minutes. After depositing her scraps in a dustbin in the kitchen, Violet smoothed down her crepe, dusty pink dress and made her way to the garden, where a quartet of stringed instruments lulled wedding guests with a mellow rendition of *Swan Lake,* by Tchaikovsky. She found an empty seat near the back.

As more guests filtered in, Violet gazed around at her handiwork, which she had finished early that morning. She had entwined the archway with grapevines snipped from thick, old vines around the pillars of the Moore home, Grapevine Lodge. She had also tucked in ivy and plumosa, pale pink ribbon, and clusters of roses, peonies, and sprays of jasmine and tulips.

Clear, glass jars were hung by silk ribbon on every other chair along the aisle and filled with a mix of the same flowers and greens. Violet hoped Holly would be pleased.

The music switched to the wedding march, and all in attendance stood as Holly walked down the grassy aisle on the arm of her uncle, whom Violet had not seen looking more attractive than he did now. Devon wore a dove-gray tuxedo, white shirt, and pale blue tie and vest, which matched the shade of his eyes perfectly. He had trimmed his goatee and mustache to a close clip, and Violet thought it made him look more dashing. Her eye caught his as he passed. Those few shared seconds lasted longer than Violet had ever known seconds to last. The pulse in her neck beat faster, and a twinge of dizziness had her gripping the back of the chair in front of her.

Passing Holly off to Matthew, Devon sat down. All the guests took their seats too.

Violet thought it odd that she'd been so focused on Devon's appearance that she had barely glimpsed Holly's wedding dress, which she now looked at the back of. The satin dress boasted tapered panels in a flattering form, all accented with light lacework. Although a lovely style, it was not the extravagant dress Violet had pictured Devon Moore purchasing for his niece. However, this understated but lovely dress suited Holly, perfectly.

The minister extolled the bride and groom and guests on the origin and meaning of love, but Violet was distracted. She stared at the back of Devon's head, and for some strange reason imagined she and Devon stood in Holly and Matthew's spots, pledging their troth to each other.

Stop it, silly! Violet chided herself. How could she

entertain a future with a man who had kept such a secret and had manipulated and lied to those he said he loved. *That was almost twelve years ago,* her conscience told her. A lot could change in twelve years, but did people change that much? Violet couldn't be certain and didn't need the kind of heartache in her life that losing her heart to a man she couldn't trust would certainly bring. Still, her gaze rested on him.

After the minister pronounced Matthew and Holly man and wife, the service drew to a close, and guests visited with each other. There were so many people Violet knew or recognized. She waved at a few people and briefly visited with others, but she didn't want to. She had too much on her mind, and large gatherings of people tended to make her nervous.

Making a polite excuse to Mrs. Dermot, Frankie's mother, whom she'd been chatting with, Violet wove through the groups of guests and went to find a seat at a table in the area of the garden where the mid-morning buffet would be served. Her stomach growled in anticipation of the sausages she had smelled and the flaky looking Danishes she had spied earlier. She should congratulate the bride and groom, but that could wait.

Stepping carefully in the grass, so as not to bury the heels of her boots in the sod, Violet sought some refuge. Just as she pulled out a chair, a voice stopped her.

"You look beautiful, Mrs. Brooks."

Violet turned, and Devon stood a few feet behind her.

He spanned the distance and met her.

Violet's fingers curled around the top of the chair she'd pulled out.

"Th...thank you," she mumbled. "Shouldn't you be with your guests?"

He uttered a light chuckle. "You're always so concerned about my guests."

He moved closer to her—too close.

Realizing she held her breath, Violet took one, working to ignore the whoosh of blood pumping in her ears. *Calm down!* she commanded herself, but with Devon so close to her she could barely breathe. She longed to reach out and run her fingers along his smooth neckline and fade into the shadow of his whiskers along his jaw. How deliciously different the two would feel.

"Violet, what happened to us?" Devon asked bluntly.

She should tell him.

Swallowing, Violet came out with it, just as blunt as he had been. "I know what happened with Holly's mother and how you deceived your family."

The skin wrinkled at the corners of his gorgeous eyes as he frowned. "Who told you?"

Violet looked him in the eye. "Holly."

He dropped his gaze, nodded, and hunched his shoulders up. "I was going to tell you, but you didn't give me a chance."

The aching tone in his voice cut at Violet.

She sensed the tension on her brow lessen, yet she demanded an answer. "How could you have done that?"

"It was a mistake and one I greatly regret, but I've changed. I'm not that kind of man anymore, one who takes what he wants."

He stood inches from her yet miles apart.

Ducking her head down for a few seconds, Violet plunged forward. "You deserve the truth—I'm...not sure I can trust you, and I'm too old to develop a relationship with someone whom I can't trust."

She hated saying the words, but her heart felt lighter having said them.

He reached for her hand. The warmth of his flesh seeped through her crocheted glove. "I know a lot more about love now, Violet. I was a fool, a stupid fool."

He gently brought the back of her hand to his mouth and kissed it. A quivering tickle spread all the way down to Violet's toes.

"Please, give me a chance to prove myself," he pleaded, his eyes commanding sympathy as well as his smooth voice. "To err is human; to forgive is divine."

Violet lifted her eyebrows, her brain ever working. "Alexander Pope, I believe."

He laughed. "Of course you would name my reference. You're the most intelligent, beautiful woman I've ever met."

He still clutched her hand. This wasn't going at all how she'd supposed. She felt her heart softening toward him.

"Other than Holly's mother, of course." Violet couldn't resist the jab.

"Those years are long gone, and Aphrodite herself stands before me."

Violet studied his eyes for any hint of deception, but she could find none. "You're too kind. Too complimentary. I'm no one to be put up on a pedestal."

"I disagree. Don't the old marriage vows say, 'With my body I thee worship?' You were meant to be adored, Violet. And if you'd let me, I would do that every day of our lives."

Violet's heart was nearly a puddle with his amorous words. *Is he proposing?* The idea of Devon and herself being married had lingered in her mind, but now that he had all but said it out loud, Violet had to make a decision. She wanted him to be clear.

"Are you…asking for my hand in marriage?"

A slow, steady smile filled with purpose spread on his face, revealing his fine teeth. "I suppose I am."

Violet honestly didn't know what to say. She looked around at the guests filtering into the dining area. Holly and Matthew entered as well, both with joyous smiles upon their faces.

Looking back at Devon and slipping her hand from his grasp, she told him, "I think we should save this conversation for another time."

Devon gazed around at the space filling up. "Yes, I believe we should." He clasped her hand again, though, as he said, "Please, don't leave without talking to me."

"You have my word, but I will need time to think."

He released her hand. "I understand." With a sideways smile of apology he continued, "Now, I must go say a few words of blessing before we begin the meal."

Violet smiled back, locking eyes with him again, experiencing that same sinking, lost feeling.

Devon moved to the table Holly and Matthew sat at. Plucking a glass of champagne off the table, he raised his voice and offered a toast, but Violet couldn't focus on his words because the words he had spoken to her jumbled around in her mind. And she was annoyed with herself for not asking about the secret admirer notes.

With this profession of love, surely, he must be the one. But something didn't sit right with Violet.

"Lord, make the way clear."

With a whispered prayer, she made an attempt to join in the celebration as best as she could.

The flower that follows the sun,
does so even on cloudy days.

Robert Leighton

CHAPTER FIFTEEN

It turned out that Violet made her apologies and went home with a headache after the wedding breakfast. She'd had a number of headaches lately, and she was tired of the strain. She gave her congratulations to the bride and groom and said goodbye to Devon, promising to see him soon and finish their conversation.

Sunday morning, Violet woke up feeling better and went to church. She needed direction, and seeking God in His house was the best place to receive that. Oh, she knew she didn't need to be in a church building to hear the voice of God, but the serene setting, the reverent hush, and the majesty of the beautiful, stained-glass windows and articles of the church reminded her of the grandness of God and that He could handle any problem of hers.

Most of the congregation left, and she sat in a pew in an almost empty sanctuary. Violet prayed quietly to herself, asking for help to know whether to trust Devon or not. She could recognize that she was strongly attracted to him, but could that be defined as love? She didn't know. Frustration built in her that as a mature woman she struggled with knowing the difference.

And can I truly love a man whom I have a difficult time trusting?

Lost in her thoughts, Violet jumped when she felt a tap on her shoulder. She turned around.

Mrs. Dermot stood in the pew behind Violet, her eyes kind, holding out an envelope. "I'm terribly sorry to intrude, Violet, but Frankie wanted me to deliver this to you."

Violet reached out and took it. For a second, she thought it was another love note, but the paper had a different texture to it. The size varied too.

"Thank you," Violet told her.

Wrinkling her substantial brows, Mrs. Dermot said, "You're welcome. I hope it's not bad news."

"As do I."

Violet pulled her lips back in a tight smile, wishing Frankie's mother would not ask any questions and leave her alone.

An awkward silence stretched between them, and Mrs. Dermot narrowed one eye and looked Violet over. But thankfully she didn't pry.

Mrs. Dermot straightened from her position leaning

over the back of the pew toward Violet and spoke in a neighborly manner. "Well, happy Sunday to you. I wish you a good day."

"Yes, you as well. Thank you," Violet replied.

She watched as Mrs. Dermot clicked away on the stone floor. Then Violet opened the note and read.

> *Dear Violet,*
>
> *I misplaced your address, so I've given this to Mother as a go-between. I have news. The shop owner wrote to me telling me that his niece did record the sale of the trap after all. Anyway, the name was a Mr. Polinski. I heard you mention that name before. It could be someone you are familiar with. I'm sorry if this brings bad news. Wishing I could be there to help you.*
>
> *Warmly,*
> *Frankie*

Violet let the letter slip from her grip. *Mr. Polinski?* The only person she knew with that name was Webster, but it couldn't be him. He wouldn't do such a terrible thing. Violet had always supposed Webster thought of her and Roger as sort of a second set of parents.

"It's not possible."

Violet spoke aloud to an empty church, her voice ringing in the void of the congregation, firm yet fearful. She took a deep breath, shook her head, and rose, the quiet spirit of prayer passing from her. Now was the time for action, and she needed to hear what Webster had to say for himself.

Determined, Violet hurried from the church and set a brisk pace in the direction of the Polinskis. She regretted her decision to walk to church. After about forty minutes, during which Violet rolled through all the possibilities why Webster would be purchasing a trap, she arrived at her neighbors'. She stepped up to the front door and knocked.

The door opened slowly, and Webster's mother appeared. "Mrs. Brooks? We don't often see you on a Sunday."

She squinted and pushed the small, gold-rimmed spectacles she wore farther up her thin nose. Fluffs of gray hair had escaped her bun, and a smile turned back her lips. Violet had always thought of Mrs. Polinski as a warm-hearted woman.

Violet clenched her hands together and went over in her head what she had settled on to say to Webster. "I was hoping to speak with Web. I have something in particular to ask him about."

Mrs. Polinski positioned her thin frame against the door to keep it open. "I'll get him for you. He's reading something, always is, if he's not in your gardens. Happens to be the almanac, today. You'd think he was an old farmer, the way he keeps his nose in that publication. Would you like to wait inside?"

Shaking her head, Violet said, "Oh, no. I'll wait out here on the porch."

"Suit yourself."

Mrs. Polinski let the screen door shut and turned, moving into the house, calling for Webster as she went.

Violet sat down in a wicker chair on the porch and made an effort to keep her heart from drumming. She turned her head when the screen door creaked open and slammed shut.

Webster ambled toward Violet, looking unlike himself, dressed in nice, dark gray pants, a white shirt, and gray, plaid tie—clearly his Sunday attire. "What? Can't get enough of me during the week? You have to come see me on Sunday too?"

He grinned in the teasing way that he had about him.

Taken aback, Violet's mind couldn't settle on what she'd planned to say. Finally, she blurted out, "I know what you did."

Blinking, Webster blushed and swallowed, his eyes on his shoes. "You worked it out, huh?"

Instead of the contriteness Violet expected in his voice, she heard something else, but she wasn't sure what. *Pride maybe?*

"Yes. I'm afraid you'll need to explain yourself."

She focused on his eyes, hoping to find regret, sorrow, any hint of remorse.

Oddly, his cheeks flushed red in what looked like embarrassment. "Well, I'd think you'd have been able to get my meaning. I thought I was pretty clear."

Anger started to bite at Violet. She stood up. "I

don't understand. What do you mean?"

He squinted and lifted his hands out of his pockets. "The reason why I did it is simple."

He stepped toward her and reached for one of her hands, but Violet pushed him away.

When she spoke, her volume and tone bordered on shouting. "And why is that?"

"I guess I gotta spell it out for you." He gave her a long, penetrating look from beneath his swath of blond hair, which had come loose from his slicked-back coiffure. His eyes pleaded with her. "I love you, Violet."

A queasiness washed over Violet. This time she truly shouted, standing up, facing him. "So you bought a bear trap!"

His face flushed a deeper red. He held out a palm. "Wait…I…I thought we were talking about the notes."

The notes? Then it hit Violet. *Good heavens, he's my secret admirer!*

She groaned. And she'd thought it couldn't get any worse.

"You wrote those?" she asked, her voice demanding, hard.

Gulping and nodding, he admitted, "Yes. I've always loved you, Violet, from the first time I saw you."

Violet flapped at the air in the space between her and Webster with both hands. "You were only ten!"

"Twelve," he corrected her, his eyes reflecting the depths of a mossy glen—the sort of place a lover's tryst might occur.

Annoyance ground through Violet. *How dare he!*

"I could be your mother."

"But you're not. Our age difference is nothing. We work so well together, Violet."

He reached for her hands, but she blocked his arms with hers. Violet felt sick and like she might vomit what little food she had in her stomach on the Polinskis' porch.

"No! Enough discussing those silly love notes!" Violet stomped her foot several times. With her burst of anger out, Violet calmed down. She spoke clearly, concisely. "You must not indulge yourself in thinking of me in such regard. I cannot reciprocate your feelings, Web." She lifted her chin and continued. "Now, let's talk about the contraption that killed Roger. Explain yourself."

She tapped her foot, hands on her hips.

Webster grimaced, looking like he'd chewed on a chokecherry. "I only set it to trap the critter that was digging up your patch of violets in the woods. I know how much you love them. Honest. I didn't mean Roger any harm." He moaned as if in pain. "It was truly an accident, and I'm sooo sorry. You must believe me."

He made to move closer to Violet, his hands held out in supplication, but she jumped back, thinking his touch would be as painful as a snake bite.

Her chest tightened as if an imaginary someone had laced her corset up with an iron hand. Then it clicked. "You mean Roger is dead because of some violets in the woods?"

Violet felt a migraine coming on.

Shrugging, his face white now, instead of red, Web said, "I...guess, but like I said, it was just to trap a varmint, nothing more."

"Why oh why didn't you say so from the beginning?" A sob caught in her throat. "You could have saved me so much worry, anger, and grief!"

He shook his head, his eyes wide and sad. His voice cracked. "I...didn't want you to hate me."

"If it truly was an accident as you say, I...wouldn't have."

Violet couldn't contain her emotion any longer and it spilled forth in uncontrollable crying. She ran away from Webster and off the Polinski property and into her backyard, but the gardens there reminded her of Webster and of Roger. So she continued running until she couldn't anymore and stopped on the road halfway to town, sweaty, tear-stained and snotty, and thoroughly unladylike. She plopped unceremoniously onto a grassy spot on the side of the road, drained.

Violet couldn't believe that Webster was the culprit *and* her secret admirer, but the more she thought about it, the more it fit. The way he'd watched her when he thought she wasn't looking. His eagerness to be the first to help. Violet had thought the language of flowers and the ardent tone of the love notes too far above a man his age, but he was an avid reader and who was to say he hadn't read poetry and the book *The Language of Flowers*? And he'd proven himself to be tender-hearted in the past.

Smoothing back her hair, Violet wiped off her perspiring face with the sleeve of her shirt. Her heart had calmed, and her head had cleared a little, which led her to thinking about how to move forward. *How can I continue to work with Web?* The question rattled her brain. No easy answer presented itself. She could let him go, but how would she manage the gardens without him? She had to come up with some solution, because she would have to face him tomorrow.

"Oh, God…" she moaned out loud and snuggled her knees up to her chin. "What should I do?"

Then an idea hit her. *What if I close the shop and go to Gwen's early?* That was perfect, almost. She would still need Webster to water the plants. But she could slip a note under his door in the evening, then pack up, hire a cab to take her to the station, and be off to Gwen's. She was sure Webster would still care for the gardens, despite what had happened between them. He was trustworthy. At least, she'd always seen him to be. But was she being a coward, running away, avoiding the issue? Probably, but Violet didn't care. She needed space to think.

But what about Devon? Violet moaned aloud. Good grief, she'd have to send him a note as well. Violet sighed, stood up, dusting off her rump, and started back home, a little lighter in spirit and thankful for the God-given inspiration to go to Gwen's immediately.

Once home she sat at her desk and penned the notes she needed to. She waited until after dark to hurry over to the Polinskis and slip the note to Webster under the door as planned. The note to Devon would be more problematic, and she hoped her delay in talking with him wouldn't sidetrack whatever progress they had made.

Next, Violet packed, watered her indoor plants, tidied up, and prepared for bed, praying that she would be able to sleep. She slept in patches but woke up feeling more clear-headed than she expected.

When washed, she ate some toast, and drank a cup of Earl Grey with an addition of lavender buds, to help soothe her nerves. Dressing in a green and purple, plaid traveling suit and pinning her favorite, violet-hued hat on her head, it didn't take Violet long to finish and to hitch up Milly and head to town. After checking Milly in at the livery and making sure she could leave her there for a few days, she hired a cabbie to the train station and paid the cabbie driver to drop the note at Grapevine Lodge. She prayed Devon would understand.

Now, she sat, tucked in a seat for the short ride to Eau Claire and to Gwen's home, banking on the hope that Gwen would help her through the recent upheaval of uncovering the truth about Roger's death and who her admirer was, all in one punch.

Violet didn't pay much attention to the loading of baggage and passengers but sat in a sort of stupor, waiting. Thankfully, no one sat near her. She had no desire to engage in conversation. Soon, the train whistle blew, the engine steamed, and the wheels began their rhythmic clickety-clacking. She let her head fall back against the headrest of the seat. Her eyes rolled shut, and in less than a minute, Violet found herself in a dense forest battling a dragon, who looked strangely like Webster, with a sword made of a bundle of gladiolus. When it seemed like she was losing, a brawny lumberjack appeared, looking suspiciously like Devon, and cut down tree after tree, allowing Violet more room to vanquish the beast.

Flowers always make people better,
healthier, happier, and more helpful;
they are sunshine, food, and medicine to the soul.

~

Author unknown

CHAPTER SIXTEEN

Having been shaken awake by the steward on the train, Violet felt rather discombobulated, but she stood and collected the large carpet bag and the brown, striped hatbox she'd brought with her. After disembarking from the train onto the platform, Violet found information about the street cars, which she'd heard Gwen mention passed near their home. Armed with directions, Violet gripped her bag in one hand and the string of her hatbox in the other and set off to test out another mode of public transportation. Her heeled boots clicking on the brick-paved sidewalk, Violet came to a streetcar junction, bought a ticket and climbed aboard.

In about three fourths of a mile, the car stopped, and she got off on Madison Street and gazed about, wondering what direction to head in, not recalling if she should take a right or left turn. Not being the best at directions, Violet was thankful she had remembered the street.

While she deliberated, Violet's gaze paused on a quaint, two-story, Victorian, cottage-style home, painted white with detailed spindle trim in dark gray and hedged in by flowerbeds. Two nice-sized maple trees reached toward the sky in the front yard.

Thank goodness. Gwen's house.

It took only a few minutes to get to the house and knock.

Gwen opened the door. Her light green, lawn shirtwaist and skirt accented her wide-open eyes beautifully.

She blinked a few times. "Violet? What…are you doing here? We expected you in a few days."

She looked past Violet, as if some explanation for her visit hung over her shoulder.

Violet steeled herself not to break down on Gwen's doorstep and throw herself into her sister's arms. "I came early. I didn't think you'd mind."

She held a sniff back and bit her lip but felt the sting of tears in the back of her throat before they wet the corners of her eyes.

Opening the stained, oak door wider, Gwen said, "Well, of course not. I'm surprised; that's all." The stupefied gape on Gwen's face switched to a warm smile. "Come in, come in."

She moved aside. Violet indulged in a few sniffs and stepped into Gwen's inviting home. Touches of comfort were all around, in the warm-toned textiles, light-painted, plastered walls, vases of fresh flowers, and tasteful accents of decor, with a definite Victorian feel.

"Thank you." Violet set her luggage down and took off her hat, hanging it up on a hook on the wall.

"Come into the kitchen, and I'll fix us a cup of tea." Gwen led the way.

Violet followed. "It's so quiet. Where are the children?"

"Melinda took Lizzy and Penny to the park. Melinda wanted to practice her watercolor painting. The little girls wished to read." Gwen placed the kettle on the stove and lit the gas burner with a strike of a match. "And, of course, Bernie is at the factory. A prominent family just put in a custom order for a whole dining set. It's one of the company's biggest orders so far this year."

Violet pulled out a small, bow-back chair at the kitchen table and sat down. "Things must be going well at the furniture shop."

"Oh, yes. The company is growing, but tell me about you." Gwen set out some cups on the table. "How did Holly's wedding go?"

Raising one shoulder and lifting one cheek in an attempt to smile, Violet said, "It was lovely."

The top of the teapot clinked as Gwen removed it and spooned in some tea. "That's all I get." She sighed and faced Violet, one eye narrow and focusing on her sister. "What about Devon? Did you talk to him? Did you ask him about that kerfuffle with Holly's mother?"

Violet reached out and fiddled with the delicate handle on the gold-trimmed teacup, painted with tiny, blue forget-me-nots. She paused as an image of Devon's perfectly sad, blue eyes came to mind. "We started to, but I left early with a headache. He…he asked me to marry him, in so many words."

"What? That was a big leap." Gwen's grin practically split her face, and her voice pitched higher. "And what did you tell him?"

Violet teeter-tottered her head back and forth. "I didn't give him an answer. I can't right now. I just found out that…"

She left her sentence unfinished, struggling to speak the terrible truth.

There was a lengthy pause.

"What? Found out what?" Gwen heaved out a sigh. "Spit it out."

She rotated her wrist and wiggled her fingers at Violet.

Violet's turmoil thickened her words. "It's Web."

She slumped in her chair, carrying the weight of her burdens on her shoulders. *Mother would tell me to give them to the Lord.*

Squinting her eyes and shaking her head, Gwen took

the kettle off the heat and poured water into the teapot. Steam rose between them. "I don't understand." Suddenly she plunked the kettle on the table and placed a hand over her heart. With her eyes wide, Gwen asked, "Is *he* your…secret admirer?"

Violet nodded.

Gwen slowly lowered herself into a chair. "Well." She rolled out the word. "He's a dark horse." She looked directly at Violet. "How do you feel about that?"

Replacing the top on the teapot, Gwen moved the kettle farther away onto a quilted pad.

"Awkward, but that's nothing to what else I have to tell you."

Gwen tucked a chunk of hair behind her ear and leaned closer. "There's more?"

Violet braved meeting Gwen's gaze. "Yes, Web is…responsible for Roger's death too."

Gwen's jaw dropped. "But he's such a nice young man and devoted to you. What happened?"

Violet filled Gwen in on the whole story, and Gwen listened without interrupting.

Gwen groaned in sympathy when Violet finished. "I'm so sorry, Vi."

Not being able to hold it in any longer, Violet let out the quiet sobs that had been clawing at her insides.

Gwen rose and came to Violet, embracing her.

Violet rested her head against her sister's middle and cried until she couldn't anymore. It galled Violet that she had resorted to tears. She hated crying, but it seemed her body had a mind of its own. And she could admit—minus her stuffy nose and head—she did feel less burdened than before.

Gwen released Violet, patting her back a few times before moving to pour the tea. "It might be a little too strong, now."

"That's fine. Do you have milk?" Violet asked.

She dabbed at her nose with the hankie she had pulled out of her sleeve. She had to have milk with black tea, strong or not.

Gwen stepped a few feet to the icebox, opened it, and withdrew some milk.

"What will you do?" she asked as she moved back to the table and poured milk from a white, enamel pitcher into a small creamer.

She handed it to Violet.

After taking the creamer and stirring in her milk, Violet confessed, "I don't know. That's why I came early, to seek your advice."

Never one to rely heavily on advice from others, Violet had done rather well so far in life, getting by with her wits and prayer, but this situation was beyond her. She couldn't think, and her prayers had been little more than brief supplications and pleas for help.

Gwen put the milk away and sat back down, pushing the sugar bowl toward Violet. "I can't say that I have anything earth-shattering to recommend." They were both silent for a few seconds, then Gwen continued, "I suppose you'll have to find a new gardener."

"Regrettably. I don't think I could work with Web after this."

Gwen took a sip of her tea then asked, "Will you involve the police?"

"Honestly, I hadn't thought that far." Violet rolled her itchy and tired eyes up to Gwen's. "Do you think I should?"

Her heart sank when she thought about Web. Honestly, she wanted to forget the whole ordeal.

Shrugging, Gwen replied, "It was an accident, and what of Webster's life? You could ruin it with the telling, if you had a mind to."

What about my vow? What about justice for Roger? Those questions rang in Violet's head, but a whispered voice kept saying, *Let it go.*

Could she, and more to the point, should she? Violet didn't contemplate further, as Gwen's girls returned from the park.

The back door slammed, and they tumbled in, pell-mell. Their eyes lit up when they saw Violet.

"Aunty Vi," Lizzy and Penny shouted in unison and scrambled to throw their arms around her.

Violet welcomed the attention and hugged them tighter than usual. "And how are the two best nieces in the world?"

"And what about me?" Melinda asked, hand on her hip, feigning a pouty lip, her smooth and dewy facial features speaking of her youth but her blossoming form telling of advancing womanhood.

Violet smiled and reached out to tweak Melinda's cheek. "You caught me. I should have said, 'Two of the three best nieces.'"

Lizzy untangled herself from Violet's neck. "Momma said you were coming for the Fourth."

Penny, with green eyes the same shade as Gwen's, tilted her head and squinted at Violet. "You're early."

Violet got lost in counting Penny's freckles for a moment. She could have sworn they had multiplied, but they still looked cute on her.

Sitting straighter in her seat, Violet settled Penny on her lap. "I am. You won't kick me out because I'm early, will you?"

Penny shook her strawberry-blonde head. "'Course not."

She giggled, covering her mouth, which boasted a missing tooth on the top.

Violet hugged her again and pecked the little girl on the cheek. "Good."

The five of them visited, and together they fixed supper. The busyness and extra bodies made Violet set aside her cares and focus on enjoying her family, something she hadn't done enough of.

Bernie came home, also surprised to see Violet, but he welcomed her graciously. Violet had always liked her brother-in-law and thought of him as kind, hard-working, and a great father and husband. A longing for Roger surfaced in Violet's heart. She missed his companionship.

Maybe I can have that again with Devon.

Experiencing the warmth of Gwen's home etched a longing in her for companionship and dared she say love?

But to see her was to love her;
love but her and love forever.

Robert Burns

CHAPTER SEVENTEEN

The days passed pleasantly at Gwen and Bernie's, and Violet almost forgot why she'd come. However, all too soon reality came calling, and the day approached for Violet to return home to her shop, gardens, and the troubles she'd left behind.

Gwen embraced Violet on the depot platform. "I know you'll do the right thing."

Violet wasn't exactly sure what that was, and she continued to pray for direction.

She leaned back from her sister and adjusted her hat. "Thanks."

Clasping Violet's hand, Gwen said, "Remember to write and let me know how you fare with everything."

"I will. Goodbye." Violet squeezed her sister's hand

one last time, let go, and got on the train, turning to wave out the window, once she'd found a seat.

The train ride back home passed by more quickly than Violet remembered. After getting off, she went directly to the livery to claim Milly, and it lifted her spirits to be rolling along behind her horse, heading home.

As she pulled into her driveway, Violet gazed around at the familiar greenhouses, gardens, and her two-story, Queen-Anne-style home. An odd sensation bubbled up in her, of happiness to be home and hope—hope that better days waited ahead.

After unhitching and settling Milly, Violet unlocked her back door and tossed her bags on the bench in the enclosed porch. She took a deep breath, and the air felt dusty and dense. Walking throughout the first floor of her home, Violet opened several windows and invited the warm, breezy day inside. Back in the entryway, she collected her things but stopped when she saw a note on the floor with the same stationery as her previous love notes. She didn't want to think about Webster and his misdeeds and misplaced affections, but she bent to pick it up and lowered herself to the bench as she opened it.

> *Dear Violet,*
>   *I am sorry for the grief and pain I've caused you over Roger's death. That was never my intention. Please forgive me for not telling you*

the truth about the animal trap. I regret every single day that I didn't. And I regret ever buying the thing in the first place.

My feelings for you have not changed, but I can clearly see my affections cannot be reciprocated by you. I realize that our working relationship will be in peril, so I've decided to give you notice of my resignation. I hope you'll be able to find a replacement.

Mother and I talked it over. With scholarships and some money she has set aside for my education, that I never knew about, I plan to study agriculture at UW Madison, this autumn.

Perhaps, some day in the future we can be friends again.

Web

Carefully folding the note back up, Violet took a deep breath and sensed a weight released from her chest. She had not come to a firm directive on whether to talk with Webster about their future, but now, it seemed that she didn't need to. Her eyes rolled closed, and she leaned her head back against the bead-board-covered wall, breathing a prayer of thanks. She surrendered her pain and her vow for the last time, and to her surprise, Violet found herself praying for Webster, that his future would not be tainted by the past.

After a few minutes of relishing the peace she felt, Violet rose to check the greenhouses and flower gardens, to make sure they had been watered. Finding all as it should be, Violet decided to select some flowers to brighten her kitchen table. Strolling along the beds, where most of the flowers were waist-high, Violet brushed her hand against them. The pungent smell of yarrow drifted to her. She clipped some stems and added them to the cutting basket draped over her arm. Next, she selected some black-eyed Susans, zinnias, cosmos, echinacea, and corn flowers.

This was where Violet belonged, here among her blooms. The comfort of it soothed her heart even more than being with Gwen and her family. Beautiful to look at and intricately unique, flowers made her happy and never failed to speak to her of God's glory and majesty.

"Solomon in all his glory…"

Violet thought of the verse in Luke 12:27 about how God would provide for the needs of his people. If He clothed the flowers in such beauty, surely, He would clothe them whom He loves most dearly.

"Was not arrayed like one of these," completed a smooth-sounding, masculine voice.

Violet spun around. Devon walked toward her, his footsteps almost silent on the cushion of mown grass.

Her heart pitter-pattered in her chest. "Devon, what a surprise."

She smiled, trying desperately to determine how she felt about him being at her home, uninvited.

His blue eyes begged forgiveness. "Sorry to come unannounced, but when I heard you were back, I had to come see you."

Stepping closer to her, Devon reached out and removed Violet's flower basket, laden with blooms. He set it on the grass.

Violet couldn't take her eyes off him. The late afternoon sun lit up his light brown, salt and pepper hair, giving it an ethereal glow, almost angelic.

In a daze, Violet spoke. "It's no problem. I'm…happy to see you."

And she was indeed. Gone were the judgmental thoughts she'd harbored toward Devon over his past. She now realized people did crazy things when they were in love, evidenced clearly by Webster.

In love. The phrase rang true to her for the first time. Seeing him, having him so close, made Violet come to the conclusion that she did love Devon Moore, past mistakes and all. Though a smidge of fear quaked in her at the thought of trusting someone—as one would trust a lover—she'd also been reminded that every person fell short at one time or another, disappointing those they loved and those who loved them. Devon deserved a second chance.

The slanted sunlight hit the curve of Devon's eyes, transforming them into blue geodes.

"I'm glad to hear you say that," he said, slow and purposeful.

With a confidence Violet hadn't seen in him before,

he circled her waist with an arm and drew her body to his, snuggling her chest against his. Being tall, Violet barely had to tip her head back to look into his eyes.

With their noses almost touching and their lips dangerously close, Violet whispered against him and asked, "You missed me, then?"

She tipped her head back enough to search his eyes, settling on the left.

Devon's other hand brushed the side of her neck, and Violet's hair stood on end with the sensation of his fingers on her skin.

"You doubted it?" he asked in the same quiet but strong voice.

Still not retreating from the magnetic pull of the blue gems of his eyes, Violet answered, "I did, but…I am willing to see what the future holds."

And with those words, Violet's spirit soared, released from the past, her broken vow to avenge Roger's death, and the way in which she had painted Devon a black sheep.

Tantalizing her, Devon's lips hovered over hers, their breath mingled. The bristle of his whiskers tickled her, sending a red-hot urge through her body that lit every nerve afire.

"That's all I need to hear," he said and without further hesitation their lips met, released and met again, deeper each time, Violet committing more than she thought she had to give.

Eventually, Devon released her lips and whispered

into her ear, "I love you, Violet."

Violet turned her head and kissed the tender part on his neck, just under his strong jaw. "I love you too, Mr. Devon Moore."

They huddled together, the cut flowers and the setting sun forgotten as they spoke and showed their ardor for each other, but suddenly, the reality that Violet had yet to tell Devon about Webster and his involvement in Roger's death came to her.

"Oh, no!" She groaned and backed away from the newfound bliss of Devon's arms around her and his lips on hers. "I need to tell you about my secret admirer and that I've found out how my late husband, Roger, died."

He released her a second, bent to pick up her basket of flowers, and nestled her in the crook of his arm.

Kissing her on the cheek, Devon said, "Tell me on the way back to your home."

They ambled toward the house, and Violet told Devon everything from the beginning, about the love notes she had received and Webster's confession of being the sender, as well as the person responsible for setting the trap that killed Roger.

Devon's eyes widened. "I'm sorry to hear that someone you trusted betrayed you in such a way, but…I can relate to the justifications and foolish actions we take when our heads are overrun with desire." With a penetrating gaze, he said, "I might have to fight a duel with this fellow, when he's back in town."

Violet shook her head but smiled, secretly gleeful that Devon would be willing to fight for her.

"There's no need for that," she told him.

They soon arrived at the kitchen entrance, and Devon opened the back door for Violet. "I wish I had thought to leave you love notes in the language of flowers."

Violet laughed and released Devon's arm, entering her home, feeling as if she were a character in one of Jane Austin's romance novels.

"To tell you the truth, I did think it was you," she confessed as he followed her inside the house.

He slipped his arm around her again. "Perhaps I'll have to try my hand at writing you one."

Focusing on his eyes, Violet said, "I think I've had enough love notes for a while, but I dream of you, here with me, and a life ahead of us, together."

"As do I."

Devon kissed her again, but Violet broke away. She pushed a hand against his chest, the light, brushed wool of his vest soft under her palm.

Running her fingers through the hair on his chin, Violet pointed out, "To be clear you haven't actually asked me to…well, you know."

She batted her eyelashes, surrendering to sentiments and female flirtations she'd thought she would never display.

He grinned, showing a line of ivory teeth. "I should remedy that."

Getting on one knee—albeit somewhat shakily—he gazed up at her and reached for her hand. All Violet could think at that moment was, *Devon Moore, one of the richest men in Chippewa Falls, is in my humble home, down on or knee in front of me!*

For a spl -second, the thought tempted Violet to compare and wonder if he'd think less of her for her modest upbringing and surroundings, but then common sense made her remember that Devon wasn't that kind of person. How much money he had did not dictate his inner qualities, the chief of which appeared to be humility.

Violet simply smiled and waited, her hand in his, with a heart full to bursting.

His forget-me-not eyes pleaded with her, and her heart melted even more.

It gave Violet pause to question herself. *When have I ever felt this wobbly inside? It's as if my innards are made of calf's foot jelly. This is what romance does to a body, apparently.* Despite her weakness, she met Devon's gaze and held it, the magic of the moment and what she knew she'd hear next building to a climax.

"Violet, will you accept the hand of a flawed man but one who has come to love you, dearly?" He gripped her hand tighter, and the strength of his fingers around hers gave Violet a sense of stability. "I promise to do everything in my power, with God's help, to show you how much I care for you, every day. I believe we fit together well, my dear, sweet, beautiful Violet. Please say you'll walk with me through the rest of this life together?"

Much to Violet's surprise, he reached into his vest pocket and pulled out a ring.

He came prepared. Violet gaped as he slipped it on her finger. It was the kind of ring she would have chosen, unconventional, understated, yet gorgeous. Around a filigreed band of gold, a center mount held a modest, beveled, rectangular amethyst; clustered on two opposite corners were tiny pearls and diamonds.

She loved it, and with tears blurring her eyes, she cried, "Yes!" and pulled Devon to his feet.

His smile split his face, stretching from one forget-me-not eye to the other. The pressure of his lips on hers felt as natural to Violet as breathing.

Buttercups have honeyed hearts,
bees, they love the clover,
but I love the daisies' dance,
all the meadow over.

~

Marjory Lowry Christie Pickthal

EPILOGUE

Three months later

Violet stood at her worktable in Fragrant Sentiments and tied plaid ribbon in an autumn color palette around the neck of an amber-colored, glass vase filled with branches of orange and red maple leaves. She made a bow with the ribbon then trimmed the tails of it on a diagonal with a sharp pair of scissors.

She glanced over at Holly. "When are you due?"

Holly placed a hand on her middle over her green apron and answered Violet, "Mid-April Doctor Kline calculated." She sighed and added two more yellow roses to what would be a wrapped bouquet, layering them in a pleasing manner, so each flower could be seen. She leaned against the wrapping counter. "I know I'll need to quit when the baby comes, but that doesn't mean I won't be bringing our little one in to visit and help out here at the shop, from time to time."

Plumping up the bow, Violet told Holly, "Well, of course, I will miss you, but my dear, I do not expect your help after the baby comes. You'll have your hands full. My niece, Melinda, will be coming to stay with Devon and I, and she'll help in the shop. She's done with normal school but will be doing a correspondence course in teaching while she's here."

"That sounds nice. I'm sure you'll enjoy her company. And I do hope that she will be a big help to you." Holly smiled, pleasant as always. "Is Uncle Devon adapting to life away from Grapevine Lodge?"

Violet thought over the last few months with her husband. "He is."

She smiled at Holly and gave a quick wink to signify all was well. *It's more than well.* Violet couldn't have chosen a man more suited to her and thanked God for directing her and Devon's paths to cross.

Violet and Devon had married quietly without any fuss with only immediate family and a few friends present. She'd held a simple bouquet of red roses and purple larkspur. Frankie had come for the wedding, and she was glad. Violet didn't wish to lose his friendship, though she had not chosen him as a suitor.

Frankie was a good sport and a gentleman and knew how to lose with grace.

With Devon gifting Grapevine Lodge to Holly and Matthew for their wedding, he had moved in with Violet. Violet hadn't objected. She felt more settled about living in her own home than a drafty lodge, and she fell more in love with Devon for his willingness to do what was best for them all.

Finishing her wrap, Holly secured the bouquet with string. "But who will you get to run deliveries?" Holly lifted the bouquet into her arms and walked toward the delivery counter. "And when is that young man coming Uncle Devon recommended?"

Violet plucked a mophead hydrangea in tones of ivory, pink, and burgundy out of a flower bucket. She made a fresh cut on the stem and added it to the vase of leaves. "Soon. Christopher worked yesterday, when you were off. He did well, and I think he'll be a good fit. He and Melinda will share the delivery tasks."

"I'm glad you found a replacement for...Webster." Holly's dark eyes widened and flicked to Violet's.

Violet was aware of the careful way Holly looked at her and spoke. Violet, of course, had told Holly why Webster had left but not every awkward detail. "Me too. Christopher is such a pleasant young man and hard-working, though he's awfully quiet. I can hardly get a word out of him."

But maybe that will be better. Violet thought it might bode her well to keep a bit of distance between herself and her new employee.

Walking back, Holly came and sat on the stool by Violet's counter. She smiled happily. "Matthew and I discussed a few names for the baby that we like. We can't decide on the boy's name, but we both like the name Daisy for a girl. What do you think, Violet?"

Adding two large, golden chrysanthemums to her arrangement, Violet echoed Holly's smile. "I love it! With the name Daisy, she's sure to be sweet, patient, and have natural beauty."

Holly chuckled. "You can tell all that from a name?"

Violet peered at her employee and niece by marriage. "My dear Holly, if there's one thing I know about, it's flowers, and that's what daisies have come to signify."

Some intuitive spirit in Violet told her that Holly and Matthew's child would be a girl and had already claimed Daisy as her name.

Violet and Holly chatted companionably, and Violet counted her blessings like flower petals falling from heaven. God had given her more than she'd asked Him for this last year: a husband who cherished her, a niece, friends, new employees, and a way to continue in business. But most importantly, the vow of retribution that had held her captive had flown away, and she couldn't be more content and at peace and hopeful for what the future held.

COMING NEXT IN
THE BOTANICAL SEASONS
NOVELLA SERIES

Daisy's Determination

Marigold's Muse

AUTHOR'S NOTE

The town of Chippewa Falls, in western Wisconsin, is real and has history in the lumber business. The term "lumber barons" was used back in the 19th century to refer to those persons who owned/operated lumber mills and made a substantial living off the lumber industry. This novella is historical primarily in the setting and time period.

Researching the floral industry during the 19th century proved difficult. I could not discover a whole lot. I did learn that one of the first retail flower shops in the United States opened in Chicago in the 1850s. Around the end of the 19th century there was a refrigeration system that some florists used. However, as I stated in *Violet's Vow*, it was expensive. Violet relied on a room built in her shop (picture a large icebox), insulated and cooled with blocks of ice to keep her flowers fresh.

Though floral techniques and styles of design have changed through the years, not much has in regard to basic flower handling. Growing and delivery have greatly expanded to large growers and spread world-wide. But the emphasis on embracing small businesses and growers in the flower industry has seen a resurgence. During my time at a local flower shop, along with the large growers and distributors, we bought product directly from local growers as well.

ACKNOWLEDGMENTS

I am grateful for the many eyes that saw and read this work before it found its way to you. My early readers and those in my Facebook group, Journeying with Jenny, have given me much support, advice, and encouragement along the way.

My family is supportive, as always, of my endeavors in authorship, and I would not be on this path of authorship without the continual strength I receive from above.

I am thankful for the help of professionals: Sara Litchfield, my editor; Jenny Q. at Historical Fiction Book Covers; my book cover designer; and Jason, my formatter at Polgarus Studio. You have all helped this book become reality. I am very grateful for each of you.

Thank you, Dear Reader, for choosing to spend your valuable time reading my words. I would deem it an honor if you could take a few minutes and leave a review for *Violet's Vow*. Your kindness would be much appreciated.

Finally, I thank God for giving me the inspiration and strength to keep writing.

Many blessings, Jenny

ABOUT JENNY

Jenny lives in Wisconsin with her husband, Ken, and their pet Yorkie, Ruby. She is also a mom and loves being a grandma. She enjoys many creative pursuits but finds writing the most fulfilling.

Spending many years as a librarian in a local public library, Jenny recently switched to using her skills as a floral designer in a retail flower shop. She is now retired from work due to disability. Her education background stems from psychology, music, and cultural missions.

All of Jenny's books have earned five-star reviews from Readers' Favorite, a book review and award contest company. She holds membership in the: Midwest Independent Booksellers Association, Wisconsin Writers Association, Christian Indie Publishing Association, and Independent Book Publishers Association.

Jenny's favorite place to relax is by the western shore of Lake Superior, where her novel series *By The Light of the Moon* is set.

Her new, historical-fiction, four-part series entitled *Sheltering Trees* is set in the area Jenny grew up in, where she currently lives, and places along Minnesota's Northern Shore, where she loves to visit.

She deems a cup of tea and a good book an essential

part of every day. When not writing, Jenny can be found reading, tending to her many houseplants, or piecing quilt blocks at her sewing machine.

Keep current with Jenny by visiting her website at www.jennyknipfer.com. Ways to connect with Jenny via social media, newsletter, and various book sites can be found on her website.